THE TOMBSTONE

Rancher Sam Crawford is renowned for his belted cattle, and his fame has spread from Texas to Montana. Unfortunately, the cattle have attracted gangs of rustlers, and Crawford has desperately sought the aid of Walt Kimball, Lincoln's town marshal. Doughty fighter though he is, Kimball deputizes young Damon Tuft to help. Danger faces the two men, and not until they encounter the mysterious tombstone of a mummified Indian will their search come to an end — but at what price?

LES LEWELLYN

THE TOMBSTONE

Complete and Unabridged

LINFORD
Leicester

First published in Great Britain in 2000 by
Robert Hale Limited
London

First Linford Edition
published 2002
by arrangement with
Robert Hale Limited
London

The moral right of the author has been asserted

British Library CIP Data

Lewellyn, Les
    The tombstone.—Large print ed.—
Linford western library
    1. Cattle stealing—Texas—Fiction
    2. Western stories
    3. Large type books
    I. Title
    823.9'14 [F]

    ISBN 0-7089-9804-6

Published by
F. A. Thorpe (Publishing)
Anstey, Leicestershire

Set by Words & Graphics Ltd.
Anstey, Leicestershire
Printed and bound in Great Britain by
T. J. International Ltd., Padstow, Cornwall

This book is printed on acid-free paper

1

Lincoln and Leesville

The reason for the placing of the village of Lincoln was elementary: there were two roads and they met where Lincoln had been established. Some kind of town was necessary to serve open country and Lincoln was no different from many others.

The people with vision who had erected the first buildings were also the ones who had little cause for complaint. They also built holding corrals.

The territory was as flat as a pancake. A person with average eyesight could see in every direction all the way to tomorrow. It was cattle country every inch of the way.

A generation or two back, Lincoln's immunity to Indian attacks was attributable to that fact.

In those days and for a while afterwards, riders on a war path made so much noise racing to the attack, by the time the broncos got within gun range, Lincoln's inhabitants were ready and waiting.

The one thing Lincoln lacked was a railroad. When it arrived as it eventually would, being flat country, the tomahawks had been pretty well run off or tamed.

In the distant mountains there were Indian *rancherias* but it had been quite a spell since any serious war-whoops had appeared painted for a fight.

Lincoln's town marshal, a bear of a man named Walter Kimball, was one of a handful of residents who remembered Indian forays. In fact it was a common opinion that old Walt Kimball and his generation were not only long past their prime but wouldn't be able to protect folks if the tomahawks came again, a remote possibility which was getting more remote as time passed.

The outlying stockmen lost a few

head from time to time, but except for raising the roof at Jake Houston's saloon and propping it up with profanity very little was done.

Until the midsummer of a particular year folks would remember, and an event, which turned out to be the reason why it was unlikely not to be remembered.

Walt Kimball heard of it three times before stirring his stumps to investigate, and even then his interest dwindled.

The Morton & Rio Grande Railroad made a sashay, kind of a loop down into the Lincoln country before straightening out and heading south-east down into the southerly border country.

At the bottom-most part of that sashay there was a sort of settlement called Leesville. Neither the skimpy settlement nor its name — Leesville to favour the Confederacy's revered Robert E. Lee — set well with the folks in Lincoln, whose name for their settlement was in favour of Abe Lincoln, the Union's head man in opposition to the Secessionist movement of the Confederacy.

But enough time had passed. Despite fierce growls against the Secesh town of Leesville nothing actually occurred of a resentful manner, except for the advent of summer weather and the establishment of that tent town down south — and one other thing.

Among the stockmen congregated at the saloon in Lincoln loudly and bitterly complaining about cattle losses and cattle thieves was Marshal Kimball with his deputy town marshal, Damon Tuft, an occasional hostler at the Lincoln livery barn and a good enough shoer of livestock, horses, mules and oxen to spell off Bud Otten, who had been shoeing for fifty years and needed a rest.

Damon was not the tallest man around but the way he was put together showed muscle where most folks didn't have the place for it. He was in his late twenties, good-natured with grey eyes and dun-coloured hair. He paid his way by doing odd jobs around town. He had cowboyed for several local stockmen and was not surprised when the town marshal wanted to hire him on for the ride to Leesville.

The reason, Marshal Kimball had explained, was because trackers hired by stockmen had dogged missing cattle to the corrals and railroad loading chute down at Leesville. As they agreed during the ride south, it wasn't possible to rustle livestock without leaving trails.

Damon did not know those folks down at Leesville had built a corral and loading chute snug up against where the train tracks had been positioned. Where the train's tracks began their sashay into the loop, the country was high enough so that when it went down to Leesville it had to slacken speed to allow for a long stretch of country that sloped south-easterly.

Leesville was lower than the country to the north-west and south-east, but the territory between Lincoln and Leesville was flat except for part of the loop. Walt and Damon had the tent town in sight half a day before they entered Leesville from the north — well — from the north-west, a smidgin more west.

It was one of those springtime days that had enough heat to it for riders to sweat.

By the time they reached the settlement they had been studying it for more than an hour.

The loading chute had been erected first; behind it was a holding corral three times the size Leesville might ever be called upon to use.

There was a store, half the size of the store where they had come from and there was a long structure made of trees so green they were still running sap.

There was another wooden structure. It was built like a bunkhouse except that it was twice as long as it was wide. A sign nailed to a tree said this was Leeville's combination saloon and eatery.

Walt and Damon looked for a livery

barn where they could put up their horses and the nearest thing they found to it was a set of log corrals. One of the corrals had animals, about equal horses and mules.

Sometime in the past, probably when the place was being constructed, there had been oxen in a separate corral. Someone had been savvy; putting oxen and horses in the same corral was an invitation to trouble. Because cattle weren't capable of getting out of the way of horses, they got chewed up; sometimes badly chewed up.

A man who hadn't been near a pair of shears — or soap — for a considerable length of time appeared with one cheek pouched out with a cud of tobacco. He smiled and agreed to care for their animals. He assured them their critters would be hayed and grained in the unoccupied corral.

Without saying his name, the livery-man told them where the town marshal's office was, said the marshal's name was Nash Bulow and led the animals away to be cared for. He also did one other thing: after the saddle animals had been looked after he crossed over to the general store to say some lawmen from Lincoln were in town looking for Nash Bulow, who was in his office which was wooden logs halfway up and canvas the rest of the way. Leesville was almost a typical railroad siding settlement, except for its means of handling cattle; and its law enforcer, Nash Bulow, had something in common with Lincoln's town marshal. Both were big, massively muscled men who, from their looks, would be capable of thinning out a den of cougars except that Marshal Bulow was a good twenty years younger than the lawman from Lincoln. He was also a brusque individual, the kind that graded his own worth to be superior to any other lawman.

As was typical of such a human being, the law enforcer of Leesville knew nothing of cattle being shipped by train from his village and preferred discussing almost anything except live-stock.

Their visit was brief; Marshal Bulow had to go north for a few days. No, he exclaimed curtly, not because of anything to do with cattle.

The Lincoln lawmen ate, wandered the tent town, spoke with several residents who would talk to strangers, and decided to head back to Lincoln.

On the ride, with the sun still burning hot but shading off to a hue of reddish light, Damon mentioned his impression of the town, its inhabitants and its lawman.

His companion listened, occasionally nodded but said very little, even less when they cut across country and found cow tracks.

Because they were both satisfied about the destination of the critters they back-tracked to locate where they had come from and, as they rode and time passed, Damon was having trouble fitting what he had seen and heard into a pattern.

Cattle was the lifeblood of their territory. They were as good as gold; in some instances they were better.

What they'd failed to discover in Leesville, among other things, was the brands on recently shipped cattle.

Cattlemen had for years lived well off yearlings and two-year-old critters, mostly steers but not always.

It was a poor stockman in their territory who did not run a minimum of a thousand mammy cows. If the price was right it was their custom to sell off only big steers and maybe keep heifers for replacements for gummer cows, or just to increase the number of their herds.

Damon was satisfied that someone was stealing cattle. The more he pondered the more convinced he became that rustling in the Lincoln country was not a pennyante proposition.

He put some questions to Marshal Kimball and received cursory answers that made him wonder if his companion was not thinking of other things, until

Kimball reined them up a long-spending rise where he drew rein with a rocky escarpment backgrounding them with a south-westerly view of grassland that ran easterly and westerly for more miles than Damon might have considered, and up there they could see riders bunching loose animals as though for a drive.

Damon knew the land, the cattle, and if he'd been closer, the riders making that gather. He rested both hands atop his saddle horn, sat like a carving in stone and was silent until the marshal said, 'Well, boy. You've worked livestock haven't you?' and, without awaiting an answer also said, 'There's part of the solution. Which way they pushing those critters?'

The answer was obvious. 'South-easterly.'

'All right, lad. Now what's south-east of here?'

'You mean what town? There isn't none for one hell of a lot of miles . . . Marshal, what're you gettin' at?'

The large older man took time to build and light a smoke before answering. 'The tent-town, boy . . . where we just come from.'

The marshal sat slouched, watching. He trickled smoke with seemingly slight concern until he said, 'Damon, you got any idea who owns that range down yonder?'

Damon replied with no hesitation. 'Sam Crawford.'

'Good boy. Now, tell me somethin' else: does Mister Crawford, or anyone else you know of, drive cattle in early summer?'

Damon sat looking far out. The only time stockmen shipped before autumn was when they were hard pressed and for a fact the cattlemen for a hundred miles in any direction did not sell down until late autumn.

In a territory like Lincoln, folks knew things; life functioned on a cycle. Damon Tuft knew as did just about everyone else how the cattle cycle worked. He grunted his reply to

Marshal Kimball and the larger man grinned around his quirly as he spoke. 'For a fact, lad. For a damned fact no one gathers an' sells down until near time for the rains to come.'

The marshal eased his horse out a tad, angling in the direction of the road. As they crossed the berm to the roadbed he smiled at his companion when he said, 'Wouldn't be much out of our way to sashay past the Crawford holdings would it?'

Damon shook his head and watched for the turnoff that led to one of the largest ranches in the territory.

They never got there. Mid-way they met Sam Crawford in his town buggy. Sam was a second generation Crawford. He was a tight-lipped individual with reddish hair who, because he was unmarried, did not shave often.

Damon acknowledged the nod and left the talking to the older men. It started out as most meetings did in livestock country. When would it rain? How much longer would the feed last?

What in hell was the president thinking of, establishing another government bureau, this time to protect the Indians and provide them with their means for survival in country where they'd been living off the land since only Gawd knew when, and ended this visit when Marshal Kimball got the conversation around to gathering and driving.

When Crawford told Walt Kimball he would not think of beginning a roundup, Damon got busy building a smoke, which he lighted as the marshal raised his rein hand to indicate the visit was finished.

Back on the road, Marshal Kimball said, 'Well, boy, I think we got our answer. Whoever's bunchin' those cattle miles back, don't ride for Sam Crawford.'

Damon was sorting through rooftops dead ahead when he replied. 'Maybe it's someone else cuttin' out his critters from Crawford's animals.'

Kimball inclined his head. 'Maybe. An' maybe somethin' else.'

14

Kimball looked gravely at his companion. 'As young as you are, boy, you hadn't ought to have such a suspicious turn of mind.'

Damon shed his smoke and laughed. 'A man gets that way accordin' to who he's ridin' with.'

Marshal Kimball nodded his head, without speaking. They got all the way back to Lincoln before the lawman said, 'I wish it wasn't so damned long a ride back to where we saw those boys gatherin' those cattle. Sure as hell, Damon, Crawford isn't gatherin' an' since those cattle we saw bein' gathered was Crawford's critters bein' bunched . . . an' Crawford don't know anything about it — '

Damon interrupted. 'But in broad daylight for Chris'sake. Marshal, Crawford's bein' rustled.'

Walt Kimball nodded. 'In broad daylight . . . Damon, are you workin' tomorrow?'

Damon put a wry look on the marshal. 'Regular pay, Marshal?'

'I expect so. After all, lad, what with folks beginnin' to be cranky about losin' cattle . . . '

'You don't want to make this ride again, Marshal?'

'Well, it's not exactly that. I've got somethin' else in mind.'

Dusk was settling when they rode as far as the livery barn in Lincoln where the marshal paid for an extra tin of rolled barley for their horses and parted company with Damon. He turned down Damon's offer to stand a round at the saloon. He had his reason so Damon hiked northerly toward the centre of Lincoln as far as the saloon and bought himself a jolt from the saloon's proprietor who had time to visit across the bar because it was close to supper-time and his trade would not pick up until his regulars had eaten supper and could sneak out and return.

Jake Houston, the saloon's proprietor, was rarely without a cigar in his face. He possessed another distinction: he used some kind of fragrant oil on his

16

dark hair, a novelty in an area where most men visited the local tonsorial parlour rarely and had their hair cut so short the tonsorial proprietor barely got by and if he'd been a family man he would not have been able to make ends meet.

Jake was good at his trade. He knew everyone's business and no one knew very much of his business. Saloon men had an occupation that just naturally invited few confidential exchanges.

He was interested in where Damon had gone today; he had seen him ride out with the marshal.

Damon was too parched to become involved in a lengthy exchange, nor did Houston push his interest. No one who was nothing more than a local handyman would be likely to be involved in anything of much interest. Handymen picked up gossip but Jake didn't need to pick that up from Damon Tuft. A saloon was by its nature an ideal institution for hearing all kinds of stories; the longer his patrons leaned on his bar the more free they became with their troubles and the troubles of others.

The only thing Damon told the saloonman that might have interested him was that on the return ride from Leesville they had seen some cattle being gathered in broad daylight on Crawford's range and when they had met Crawford he had not mentioned starting to gather.

Jake scoffed at Damon's implication of rustling. 'From Crawford's range right under his nose, Damon? Naw; he must've sent riders out to start his annual roundup early, an' forgot all about it.'

Damon had two jolts under his belt and the third one in the small glass in front of him when he agreed with Houston, particularly when Houston off-handedly said he'd noticed Crawford being absentminded lately.

They embarked on another subject; the weather. If there was one topic worth discussing in ranching country it was when the next rainfall would arrive. They finished discussing this prospect after Damon had finished his third jolt and was ready to leave.

2

The Trail

It was customary for unmarried range-men, owners as well as their riders, to visit May's café in town. In fact almost any day, with the possible exception of Sunday, May did a lively business, not because of her female charms. She was a widow woman who weighed close to 200 pounds and was in her fifties but in a coarse, direct way May was not above flirting, something both May and her regulars made many a private joke about.

She and Marshal Kimball had been skirting around this issue of both being single for some time. The marshal with a room out back of his jailhouse couldn't cook toast nor boil water for coffee without burning it. He budgeted his wages to include two meals a day at

May's eatery and was having breakfast, the last early diner of the day, when Leonard Holt came in looking ruffled, sat down next to the marshal, ordered fried eggs and spuds, and waited until May had gone to her kitchen before he leaned toward the marshal and spoke in a gravelly voice lowered so he could not be heard as he told the local lawman Sam Crawford liked to have had a seizure. He had driven out in his buggy as he often did to make a rough tally of how much of a selldown he could make in a few months when autumn arrived. Leonard leaned closer. 'He come back roarin' mad . . . he come up short some hundreds of yearlings an' long yearlings he expected to sell off this Fall. Marshal, I got to tell you, I've worked for Sam close to ten years an' in all that time I've never seen him fired up like he was yestiddy when he come back from goin' out among 'em. He was so upset he liked to had a stroke.

'He told me last night after supper to get the hell over to Lincoln an' tell you he's bein' rustled blind.'

May brought Leonard's eggs and spuds, winked at the marshal and with a hippy stroll went back to her cooking area. The marshal did not say a word until Leonard had finished his breakfast and had placed the two-bit coin beside his plate and reared back to arise. He knew Leonard Holt, Sam Crawford's forty-a-month range boss. He waited until May had come for the plate and the coin, looked from one of them to the other and addressed the rangeman. 'Leonard, if you was keepin' your voice low, don't you never come in here talkin' in your normal voice.'

May put both hands on her hips, looking fiercely at the rangeman. 'How many head?'

Leonard shuffled his feet, raised his eyes and answered, 'All's he guessed was about fifty, sixty head. Both steers an' heifers. You couldn't hear me back yonder, May.'

She snorted, gathered the plates and marched away without a word.

Leonard left the eatery in favour of Houston's waterhole where to his disappointment there was only Jake and a nearly deaf early starter at the bar.

May shook her blonde hair at the marshal. 'If Sam Crawford was rustled of sixty head I won't shed a tear. Walt, you goin' out there?'

'I was out there a week or so ago, me'n Damon.'

'That don't answer me, Walt.'

He got to the door before speaking. 'No.'

Fed and ready for the day, the marshal was studying Wanted dodgers, just about the only thing he received in the mail, when Sam Crawford came in, glared and sat on a wall bench, pushed out his legs and said, 'Walt, I been rustled of about fifty, sixty head of critters ready to get drove south.'

Kimball settled more comfortably in his desk chair. 'When?'

'All I know for a fact it was within the last few weeks.'

'Did you dog 'em, Sam?'

'I only just discovered it yestiddy. I got a rider who claims to be a tracker skulkin' around until he picks up the sign.'

'When did you send him out?'

'Well, this mornin' early.'

Kimball leaned back off his desk, intertwined his fingers and showed an almost cherubic smile. 'You remember that day me'n Damon met you?'

'I remember. Ten days ago for a fact. What about it?'

'On our way back to town,' the marshal said, 'we saw some fellers gatherin' cattle on your range near where that fallin' down squatter shack is.'

Crawford jerked straight up in his chair. 'The old Mallory place.'

Kimball leaned forward on his desk. 'Looked to be maybe about thirty, forty head, Sam. They was doin' a good job. They turned back gummer cows, bulls, an' cut out skinny butcher animals.'

'You just watched, Walt?'

'Makin' a gather on your land, Sam,

they could have been your cattle as near as I could make out. They could have been doin' what you told 'em to do.'

Sam Crawford had to be satisfied with that. He shifted again in the chair before speaking. 'Too far to make things out good, Walt?'

Kimball nodded. 'Too far, Sam.'

As Crawford got to his full height he said, 'If you was to pick up their sign, Walt . . . ?'

'Maybe in a few days, Sam. Right now I'm about snowed under.' The lawman also arose. He held the roadway door open. 'Sam, anythin' you or your riders pick up, I'd take it right kindly if it was brought to me.'

Crawford nodded in the doorway. 'But I'll do some doggin' too.'

'Good luck, Sam.'

After the cowman had departed, Marshal Kimball went walking down to the livery barn, asked the liveryman if he had seen Damon. The liveryman jerked his head and said, 'Out back, rubbin' down a horse.'

Damon nodded as the marshal walked up and motioned him to a horseshoe keg from which the lawman removed a pair of horseshoes sitting on top and sat down.

After Marshal Kimball related what Sam had said and that he wanted Damon as deputy again, Damon asked, 'Is there a reward?'

Kimball shook his head. 'There isn't far as I know. Damon, don't go and get greedy on me. When you backtracked those cattle we saw, did they use the train?'

'I told you, they drove 'em.'

Crawford moved on the keg to avoid being stuck in the tail by a splinter. He arose, dusted his britches and said, 'Good job, Damon. Did you pick up any names?'

'One: Owen. I don't know whether it was a first or a last name.'

'Just Owen, no other name?'

'Just Owen. He was one of the riders. What he said the riders did. Big feller, about your size. Had a little age on him.

When anyone gave orders it was him — Owen.'

Kimball put on his hat and said, 'Three-day ride, is it?'

'More like four days.'

Marshal Kimball got as far as the livery barn's roadway door before he stopped and spoke. 'Same pay, you lead off.'

'Marshal, I can draw you a map.'

Kimball shook his head. 'Same pay an' you lead the way.'

'Marshal, I haven't been paid yet. You pay me up to date an' I'll take you to their damned front yard. Marshal, what do you think of taking a posse, I got no idea how many there are.'

'You mentioned four an' that's what I counted when we was on the ridge watchin' them.'

Damon had a reply ready, but as he looked at the large man he let it die. Instead he said, 'In the morning,' and after Kimball had walked away Damon let go a long sigh, went to take his shellbelt and holstered Colt from a wall peg and carefully examined them both.

While he was doing this an old man who swept out for the saloonman came along to relay a message. The saloon proprietor wanted Damon to repair a door some drunk fell against. 'Tomorrow,' the swamper said. 'First thing in the mornin'. I can't imagine him not bein' able to lock up.'

Damon off-handedly nodded. Not until the swamper was gone did he remember he would be riding out with the marshal the following morning.

He had a few chores to do before morning and embarked to do them.

The liveryman wasn't surprised to see Damon graining his horse. To the liveryman that meant Damon would be going somewhere a-horseback.

He was heading for the eatery with the sun almost gone when he encountered the saloonman who stopped Damon at the café's entrance and explained about his broken door.

Damon was on the verge of explaining why he would not be able to fix the door until maybe day after tomorrow when Marshal Kimball came up, slapped Damon lightly on the shoulder and said, 'I'll stand supper,' and with a nod to the saloonman herded Damon inside where two old men were slurping tan-looking bean soup and sat at the furthest end of the counter. May appeared, Kimball ordered for them both and after May returned to her kitchen he said, 'If it's very far, Damon, maybe we'd ought to head out tonight. Not wait for dawn.'

Damon shook his head. 'In the morning,' he said, as May appeared with two thick bowls of that bean soup to tide them over until she had supper ready.

The marshal dourly grunted. He was not an accomplished sleeper.

After they had eaten and parted company outside, Kimball went in the direction of the saddle and harness works. He and the leather-shop proprietor were cribbage players. It was a years' long custom; they played on every Friday night after the harness man closed up his shop.

On the wall above his cutting table, the leather man had a homemade sign that said, 'Trouble Comes In Double'.

Marshal Kimball had barely got seated in the harness works when a rawboned man carrying a saddle began beating on the roadside door.

When the leather man ignored it, the stranger beat on the door with a big closed fist.

The harness maker rolled his eyes at the marshal and went to the door.

The stranger came in, lightly flung his saddle atop the counter and rolled back a fender and latigo ring. 'Broke,' he said. 'I got no idea where or when. Alls I know, I was ridin' up a slope an' the rig kept slidin' back on me. About when I slowed to feel around, off we went, me'n the saddle. Look there, mister, that saddle is less'n three years old. See that riggin' leather that goes up under and comes down around the cinch ring, broke neat as though it was cut.'

The saddle man roughly up-ended the saddle, examined the damage and said, 'A coupla days, mister. The underlayin' rigging strap is busted. I got to take the whole rig apart to put in another one.'

The stranger scowled. 'Can you patch it with rawhide?'

The saddler looked shocked. 'Rawhide? Mister, you never built a saddle, did you? A man can't make that repair usin' rawhide.'

'Well . . . somethin' that's just as tough?'

The saddler's expression softened. 'Yeah, but I can't get to it for a coupla days.'

The stranger didn't look appeased. 'Not tomorrow?'

'Mister, I got a set of chain harness to fix for the feller runnin' the stage, an' a saddle with busted swells, for tomorrow.'

The stranger shifted his feet, dug deep into a trouser pocket and brought forth a wad of high-denomination greenbacks. Slowly he peeled off one and looked up. The saddler gave his head a gentle wag.

The stranger skived off another greenback. The saddler looked up at him, smiled and held out his hand. The stranger held out his hand holding a pair of twenty-dollar bills. The saddler took them, said, 'Tomorrow,' and sat down to play cribbage.

The marshal made a wry comment. 'Remember coupla years back when you replaced a riggin' like that for me?'

The saddler did not look up when he said, 'That's different, Walt. We been friends a long time. For you it was two dollars.'

The marshal gave an exaggerated wag of his head and said no more until Buck Thorne, owner of the general store, came over as Marshal Kimball was about to leave, loser again. Thorne caught hold of Kimball's arm. Buck was agitated, which wasn't exactly a novelty, he was a storekeeper.

He said, 'Marshal, there's a feller

over at the saloon. I swear I've seen his likeness on the wall at your office.'

The leather man closed the door. It was past his bedtime. The storekeeper paid no attention. 'Marshal, if you'll come along I'll stay by the doors an' nod my head when you're near the feller.'

Kimball did not move. He asked the man's name and the storekeeper did not know it so he repeated his earlier offer. He would let the lawman know when he was close.

The marshal stolidly considered the store man. 'Buck, I'm not goin' to barge in over yonder an' grab someone you think is an outlaw. Let me tell you what happened to an uncle of mine down in Texas years back who did somethin' like you expect I'll do. He got shot in — '

'Marshal! I'm sure it's the same man as you got a dodger on in your office.' The storekeeper gestured. 'If it ain't I just won't raise my arm. Mr Kimball, I don't expect that feller to stay at the bar until Christmas. Are you comin' or not?'

The marshal reached, gave the storekeeper a light shove and said, 'Let's go.'

When they crossed the street and halted out front of the spindle doors, Buck Thorne gestured for Kimball to go inside and took a position outside where he could watch the marshal's progress. A misfire was not unusual. Two rangemen were standing at the bar which was fairly crowded; the store-keeper vigorously nodded his head in their direction.

Kimball knew one of them, he hauled freight to several towns and his name was Jim Harper. Kimball tapped him on the shoulder. When Harper faced around broadly smiling, the man beside him also turned. He looked at the marshal, nodded, moved around him away from the bar and roughly pushed his way past the swivel door where the storekeeper was standing. Buck Thorne moved away, watched the man who had bumped him untie a horse at the hitch rack, mount and rein northward at an easy lope.

Thorne pushed past, got inside and approached the marshal scowling. 'You got the wrong man, damn it. He just now came out, got on his horse and left town northerly.'

The smiling townsman Kimball had tapped on the shoulder looked from one of them to the other, stopped smiling and was turning back to the bar when he growled, 'Buck, what'n hell are you up to? Marshal, I'll stand you a round.'

Marshal Kimball said, 'Thanks, another time,' took the storekeeper in a grip of iron and escorted him out of the saloon. The proprietor, who had witnessed everything, leaned on his bar and cursed under his breath.

The night was moving along, but Marshal Kimball paid it no heed as he pushed Buck Thorne against the rough outside wall and said, 'You danged fool. Someday you'll do somethin' like that an' you'll get somebody killed.'

The storekeeper continued to stand against the rough boards unnoticed by several patrons departing from the saloon.

When he was about to leave, the saloonman came out, saw him and said, 'Buck, he came in, walked up to one of the local freighters an' tapped the wrong man. The feller you was supposed to point out walked right past an' left. You got somethin' to say for yourself?'

The storekeeper did have. He said, 'Good night,' and went scuttling towards his store.

The marshal went along to the rooming-house, met the proprietor sitting on the porch smoking his pipe and eased down in another chair. The pipe smoker said, 'Nice, quiet town, Marshal.'

Walt Kimball agreed without even a pinch of insincerity and after a short rest on the porch he went hiking on to his room in back of the jailhouse, shucked out of his boots, put his shellbelt and holstered sidearm on a table, dropped his hat on the floor and within moments of lying flat out was sound asleep.

What awakened him was Damon Tuft rattling the door. Kimball went in his stockinged feet to unlock the door, recognize who his caller was and went to the only chair to tug into his boots as the younger man said, 'It'll be sun-up in another hour. If we got an early start it might help. We'll be doggin' those rustlers through some almighty thick timber.'

The marshal arose to stamp his feet. He also drew forth from his pocket a large, thick gold watch. He consulted its face, repocketed it, wordlessly hitched into his gunbelt and reached for his hat before speaking. 'Last night you didn't want to get an early start.'

Damon went to hold the door open, watched the marshal blow out the light and said, 'Changed my mind. Got to thinkin' about the distance an' if we catch 'em tomorrow night in the dark we might surprise 'em, get the drop on 'em.'

Kimball nodded his head, dropped on his hat and walked past the younger man as he said, 'Let's go.'

There was no need to waken the liveryman, who slept in his harness room, so they got rigged out and led their horses outside to be mounted.

They didn't lift over into a lope for almost two miles which gave their animals plenty of time to be warmed out.

It was one of those late springtime nights when there was a lingering sense of a dying warm day before a hint of a still-cold leftover winter chill.

Damon was bundled in a rider's coat someone had given him. It was lined with sheep pelt. A man could stand just about all the night-riding he felt obliged to do. The marshal had a similar rider's coat but being close to twenty years older some cold could penetrate.

As soon as they left open country and

had to work their way northward on a sashaying course it was less the cold than it was the variety of darkness two night riders had to pass through into an unknown.

At times they were separated by a fair distance. The marshal seemed to require reassurance. He saw no tracks until dawn's precursing long thin shaft of predawn light helped visibility.

Three times the marshal got close enough to be reassured. After the third time he could make out enough sign to require no further assurance. Damon knew where they were and where they were going.

3

Shipman's Meadow

Walt Kimball had been the local law in one place or another for more years than his companion was old. Rustlers were no novelty to him but the further they went as the new day brightened around them the more puzzled he became.

With full daylight, reading the sign of a passel of hooved animals passing in and out of timbered terrain increased his bafflement. He said nothing of this to his riding partner until they broke clear of trees with a large sprawling meadow ahead — with hungry cattle on it, cropping feed like there would never be any more.

The marshal drew rein while he still had a backdrop of trees and said, 'Boy, you know old Crawford's mark?'

Damon answered immediately. 'Bar SC. You can't make it out from here.'

'Don't have to,' the older man retorted. 'You see a belted critter nearer us westerly?'

This time the reply came slower. 'Well . . . I can't see her far side from here.' Damon raised an arm to point. 'Got a white belt as much as I can see. Walt . . . ?'

'Well, a few years back Sam Crawford got this crazy idea. He found three belted cows, had 'em corralled, had bulls drove into the corrals with 'em, an', boy, that's what you're lookin' at. Let's angle around in the trees until we can see the other side.'

The sun climbed, slowly for a fact but inexorably. By the time they got far enough north-westerly the marshal said nothing when Damon made a low whistling intake of breath. The same heifer had the other half of her belt showing on the far side. She looked freakish among critters of solid colour. She didn't know it and neither did any

41

of the other cattle.

Kimball said, 'Well, that settles it for me. How about you?'

It settled things for Damon, not entirely because of the belted cow, but also because tracking had led them here. He did a little sashaying, enough to see other brands. Every critter had a Bar SC on the right side.

Walt looped his reins to roll and light a smoke. Damon did too but he wasn't silent. He said, 'Smoke risin' from the stovepipe, Walt.'

Kimball lighted up and nodded on the exhale. 'The question is — how many rustlers is up here?'

Damon answered that with conviction. He was as accomplished a sign reader as there was in the territory. 'Four,' he said, resting both hands on his saddle horn. 'Wait until they come out. Maybe one at a time.'

Walt neither agreed nor disagreed, he simply swung to the ground facing the distant cabin. As he looked around for a low limb to tie his horse to he said,

'That's good odds, Damon. But if they're old hands things might get sticky.'

Damon sank to one knee and trailed the reins over a shoulder. 'Tell you what, Marshal. I'll ride over there. Me alone. Make up a story before I get there.' Damon looked up and wryly smiled. 'Just another saddle tramp.'

Walt did not say what he thought; if anyone could rightly pass as a saddle bum it was his companion. Runover old boots, creek-washed old faded work-shirt. Britches patched at one seam and snagged but not sewn on the other leg, an old scarred holster with a smooth-worn old Colt six-gun.

Walt nodded, almost anyone would guess his riding partner to be a free-loader if there was ever one who looked the part.

He took the reins, tied Damon's animal and turned back. Damon had arisen and was scowling. 'I dassn't go over there on foot.'

Walt coloured, led the horse back

and handed over its reins. As he moved clear he did not look up when he said, 'Be real careful, Damon. They didn't drive them critters far enough not to be tracked. I'll see about slippin' around back. If you get 'em outside I'll do the rest.'

Damon nodded, took the reins, nodded curtly and started riding. Part way across the grassy big clearing he told his horse the marshal was getting absent-minded. It was also getting close to the time for a man to sit in the shade somewhere and whittle.

There was a wisp of movement around in front of the cabin. A man appeared partly shadowed by shade, the next second he had ducked back inside.

Damon smiled to himself. He hadn't expected to surprise anyone but he hadn't expected to be discovered when he was still more than ten or twelve yards from the house.

Sunlight bounced off the blue steel barrel of a Winchester saddle gun out past a movable slat that served as a window.

Damon fished into a shirt pocket, brought forth a battered mouth organ and began playing *Danny Boy*. The musical instrument had its share of dust, lint and something else that prevented it from producing acceptable music.

The horse bypassed some cattle who threw up their heads as he passed, then went back to grazing with no interest in the mounted man making strange sounds.

A tall, thin man came out of the old shack. He stood like a statue for as long as he required to make some kind of judgement, then he stepped back and called.

'Pete! We got us a visitor.'

The second man to come out was shorter, wore a black hat pulled low in front like he was accustomed to riding into the sun, who wore his holstered six-gun low on the left side of a shellbelt that also held a skinning knife in an elegantly beaded sheath. This man had a cud in his cheek that was noticeable a fair distance.

No one else came out of the cabin. As Damon got closer he could see the lodgepole pine corral on the north side. He could not see one side of the house but what he could see had two horses in the corral standing close and also watching Damon approach.

He and the marshal had tracked four riders. As Damon got closer he speculated. The missing rustlers might be back-tracking or they might have gone to some rendezvous. He had no time for a lot of speculation. The tall rustler called a greeting, 'Howdy, neighbour.'

Damon responded in a slightly raised voice. 'Howdy, friend. You wouldn't have some beans an' creek water would you?'

The tall man smiled broadly. 'Put up your horse. We can likely scare up somethin'.'

Damon looked as affable as the tall

man also seemed to be, but his short-ribbed companion worked his cud and said nothing. He went back inside.

The tall rustler walked to the corral with Damon, leaned on the stringers while watching Damon shed his outfit and linger long enough to see his horse get down and roll, first on one side then on the other side. The tall man said, 'Worth forty dollars,' and laughed as Damon approached the gate.

It was an old joke. For every time a horse could roll over and back he was worth twenty dollars.

Damon shoved out his hand. 'Jim Hubble,' he said. As the tall man reached to shake he introduced himself. 'Charley Oden. Feller inside is Pete Forchay. He'll be rasslin' you somethin' to eat. Me'n him already ate.'

As they strode for the front door, which faced east, he also said, 'You ride for someone hereabouts, Jim?'

Damon showed a bland smile. 'Haven't found no work all year.'

Charley's smile knowingly broadened. 'Ridin' the grub-line trail?' and Damon made a rueful grin.

'Good guess, Charley. You ever try it?'

'Couple of times.' Charley's smile lingered. 'Liked to starved to death both times.'

Inside what had once been someone's line shack was surprisingly clean and orderly. There were two bunks on opposite walls, an old-time barracks heater, wellstocked shelves, a crudely made table with four benches and some neatly piled kindling.

The other rustler was making a meal at the black iron stove and turned long enough to introduce himself as Pete Forchay.

He was busy at the stove as his companion got Damon settled on one of the little benches and asked questions, not wary questions, general questions.

When Damon had seemed to have satisfied the rustler called Pete he said something about the cattle grazing off the big meadow and Pete Forchay interrupted by bringing a dented metal plate of food and to also ask questions which Damon answered between mouthfuls. The meal was better than Damon had eaten in many professional eateries, and he said as much, which Pete seemed to take in stride. He told Damon that making good meals out of cow country gatherings was his hobby. He also said something else that stopped Damon's knife from reaching his mouth as he spoke. 'Your big old friend wouldn't like to also eat?'

Neither of the rustlers smiled as they put aside their cups of coffee and stared unwaveringly at Damon.

The man who had said his name was Charley made a slight noise sucking his teeth but his partner neither moved nor blinked in his regard of Damon.

Damon was naturally quick-witted but just barely this time. Pete had caught him entirely unprepared. Charley shattered the long silence by continuing to suck his teeth.

Charley and Pete sat facing each other north and south. Damon had his back to the door, facing the cabin's west wall, the one with the movable slat that served in very hot weather as a window.

Damon saw it move a fraction. His eyes unconsciously widened and Pete noticed. He was leaning forward to arise, his right hand out of Damon's sight when the slat moved wide and the face in the opening spoke. 'Touch that gun you bastard an' I'll blow your gawddamn head off.' Forchay was half standing, half leaning.

'Put your hand where I can see it!'

Damon was rooted. He had never been as glad to see Walt Kimball's lined and weathered face in his life. He looked at Pete as he said, 'You heard him. *Do it*!'

Very carefully Pete raised his hand and laid it atop the table and very slowly and carefully sat back down.

The marshal said, 'Watch 'em,

Damon. Get their guns!'

The face disappeared and the back window slat dropped back into place. The rustler called Charley looked almost reproachfully at Damon. They both saw Damon's gun rise and obeyed; they lifted out their sixguns and very gently placed them atop the table.

When Walt Kimball appeared in the doorway, gun in hand, he looked giant-size and hostile. He glared at Pete. 'What in hell do you think you're doing? I thought I recognized you.'

Pete sat riveted to his bench returning Kimball's stare. When he could speak he said, 'What in hell is goin' on, Marshal? We seen you two back-trackin' us.'

Kimball snarled. 'Where's the other two? We tracked four of you.'

Pete answered promptly. 'They went back. Len an' that new man, I forget his name.'

The large-appearing hostile lawman in the doorway seemed to perceptibly loosen. 'Leonard . . . was in on this, you rustlin' pair of sons of bitches?'

This time the tall rustler spoke. 'Marshal, you know me?'

'No. Well, I've seen you on Sam Crawford's place and maybe in town. What of it; am I supposed to know you?'

The tall, thin man put his attention on Pete. 'Somethin's . . . Pete, what in hell . . . ?'

Pete did not allow him to finish. He relaxed at the table, seemed to be pondering and eventually addressed Marshal Kimball.

'You dogged us?' he said and leaned with both elbows on the table. 'Mind tellin' me why?'

'Because I never could stand rustlers, that's why!'

For several seconds the shack was as quiet as a tomb before Pete explosively said, 'Rustlers!' He would have said more but Walt also exploded.

'You damned idiots . . . rustlin' cattle from the man you work for!'

The tall man raised his hat, resettled it and looked round-eyed at Pete, who straightened where he sat. 'Rustled! Rustled Sam's cattle . . . you idiot, we work for Sam. He had this bunch cut out some days back, then he sent the range boss and us with him to drive these critters up here to Shipman's Meadow.'

The silence returned and lingered. Very slowly Walt Kimball holstered his six-gun after easing the hammer down very gently. Most of the stiffness left him as he looked from the tall rider to Pete. When he spoke his voice was scratchy with bafflement.

'Sam had this bunch cut out an' drove up here?'

'Yes . . . you gawddamned idiot! An' we saw us bein' followed but paid it no heed. You thought we was stealin' them cattle?'

Walt nodded slightly. 'What else was we to believe? Mister . . . what's your name?'

'Pete Forchay.'

'How long you been workin' for Sam Crawford?'

'About a month. Why?'

'Because I never saw you in town. Not that I recollect anyway.'

Pete crossed to the stove where he opened the fire box and jettisoned his cud. As he faced back around he said, 'Mister, I come with a band of bred-up heifers that Sam bought down south. That's how come me to work for him. I don't think I ever seen you either.'

Pete marched back to his bench and sat down angrily, looking steadily at the town marshal. 'You're Kimball, the town marshal?'

'Yes.'

'I've heard of you. This here young feller . . . ?'

'Right now he's deputyin' for me. His name's Damon Tuft.'

Pete Forchay groped in a pocket for what remained of a plug of Mule Shoe, worried off a fresh cud and cheeked it. He did all this and repocketed the chewing tobacco without a word, but after the remnant was pocketed he spoke.

'Somethin' here I'm havin' trouble with. You'n him saw us movin' that little band of Crawford cattle, figured we was cattle thieves and dogged us to this place, which Sam's range boss called Shipman's Meadow. Am I right, Mr Kimball?'

'Right as rain, Mister Foochee.'

'For-chay.'

Walt briefly reddened. 'Mister Forchay . . . that's plumb right. We seen some riders a few days back with them prime critters north of town on Sam Crawford's land. This here is about all the land around here Sam don't own . . . an' they wasn't just any critters, they was prime, the kind a cowman'd keep back from a drive to rail's end down south some distance. Now then, Mr Forchay, what was we supposed to think? Riders bunchin' Bar SC cattle. Prime animals to their owner or to enterprisin' rustlers.'

Pete had the answer and he gave it.

'Marshal, before I'd dang near get some fellers shot I'd've rode over an' asked Sam whose cattle they was an' did he want 'em bunched for the drive to this meadow.'

There was enough to what Pete Forchay had said to keep Walt leanin' in the doorway speechless. He eventually drifted his gaze to Damon as though there could be a possibility for placing the blame for Walt's blunder in Damon's direction.

Damon returned the lawman's look for a moment then mentioned something totally irrelevant to this situation where someone had come within an ace of getting shot.

'Marshal, this here mulligan stew or whatever it is, goes down real easy.'

As irrelevant as the statement was it was correctly oriented in the direction of men whose stomachs were near enough to being empty to being relevant. The tall rangeman, Charley Oden, made a friendly gesture toward Walt Kimball. 'Mister, there's four benches . . . Pete?'

Forchay considered his companion, let go a big sigh and arose to head for the stove and another dented old tin plate. As he worked over there he said, 'Marshal, maybe you can unwind some of this for me. Why'd Sam get us to cut out this bunch and bring 'em up here?'

Kimball, who was a stomach-oriented lawman was straddling one of the rickety benches when he answered without looking up. 'He wanted this bunch cut away from other critters . . . maybe to keep 'em away from a regular nucleus of a seasonal drive.'

Damon put down his knife. 'What kind, Walt?'

'A nucleus,' Kimball replied and paused in his masticating to explain its meaning.

'He wanted them apart so's the others wouldn't smell 'em and go where they was, mostly critters that'd scent-up bullin' heifers.'

That conversation died right there. The tall rangeman Charley Oden, repeatedly mumbled that word he'd never heard before. The others ignored him.

When Kimball was full as a tick he used a large blue bandanna to clean his hands and face, then went out to see how his horse was getting along and Pete Forchay followed him. There was loose-cut fragrant timothy hay in a three-sided lean-to off the corral. Pete knew where the fork was and spoke as he handed it to Walt.

'I'm havin' trouble with this, Mr — '

'Kimball. Just plain Walt. It sticks in my craw too but then I was never a rangeman.'

Pete watched Walt pitchfork feed which the corralled animals went after like they did not believe there would ever be any more. 'Guess there's nothin' to puzzle over, Walt. Mister Crawford wanted these prime beeves cut away from what he otherwise figures to sell.'

Walt finished forking feed, leaned the fork aside and faced the swarthy man who wore a fleshing knife twenty years after most rangemen had given it up.

'Is it usual with Sam Crawford, Mr Forchay?'

'Pete. Just plain Pete. Is what usual with Sam?'

'Cuttin' out and drivin' off a fair-sized bunch of prime beef to get 'em away from other cattle?'

Pete leaned on a corral stringer and watched the horses eat as he answered. 'Well, no, it's not usual with most cowmen, but I only been here a month. That's not long enough to get a boss's savvy.'

Walt agreed by nodding as he also said, 'Them other two fellers who helped you push those critters . . . was this common to them?'

Pete slowly twisted to face the marshal. 'No, I think not. Leonard, the foreman, rode with me and cussed every foot of the way. They was supposed to be puttin' up hay for winter-feed. He said old Sam's gettin' harebrained to want them prime critters cut loose and pushed up here.'

As they walked back to the line shack, or whatever the little cobbled-together log-and-slab cabin was, the marshal said nothing until they were within reach of the latch string, then he stopped the other man with a question.

'Is Sam gettin' close to makin' a gather for a drive to rail's end like he's done ever since I've been here?'

When Pete replied he sounded annoyed.

'Sam'll run his outfit any way he wants to. Yes, that's why he wanted Len an' the others at the home place. To start gatherin' for cuttin' out what stays and what goes. It's a tad early accordin' to what Len said, but Walt, cowmen didn't get big outfits by copyin' other folks. You wouldn't have a snort or two in your saddlebags would you? Right now I'd trade five years off my life for a healthy snort.'

Walt grinned and lightly slapped the shorter man on the shoulder. 'Used it all up before we come up here.'

4

Sam's Ride

No man liked to be made a fool of and Pete Forchay was no exception. When they got back inside where it was warm, almost too warm, and someone had turned down the damper, he tossed his hat on one of the wall bunks, scratched heartily and wagged his head in the direction of the table where three men sat, and said, 'Somethin's botherin' me. Sam Crawford owns them cattle outside. Bein' the owner he's got the right to put his critters any place he can. Me'n Charley work for Mr Crawford; he told us to mind these cattle which is what we figured on doin'.'

Pete did not join the others at the table, he sat on the edge of his bunk giving Walt Kimball look for look.

He was waiting; it wasn't a long wait.

Walt explained how and why he and his companion were up there. The more he talked the more it struck even him as the speaker, how awkward he sounded. He closed his remark with one long sentence. 'Pete, we watched some Crawford riders workin' those cattle some days back. Right now I think what we saw was those critters being drove their first day's hike up to this big meadow.' As he spoke an idea occurred to the lawman. 'Suppose come mornin' you'n me ride back an' get Sam Crawford to untangle this mess.'

Pete Forchay was kicking out of his boots when he replied, 'Won't be necessary. Sam an' Len are due up here tomorrow.' As Pete freed-up his shell-belt and curled it to be placed near where his head would be when he bedded down, he prepared to shed his shirt when he spoke tiredly. 'Marshal, you know Crawford's other riders?'

Walt had to ponder. The village and its surrounding territory was livestock country miles further than a man could see. He could name the owners but not every rangeman. Riders came and went.

Walt reluctantly shook his head. 'I know some of 'em,' he told Forchay. 'The old hands; an' maybe most of the boys who hire on every spring, but, mister, it's a big territory with lots of cattle an' dozens of hired hands.' After a brief hesitation he also said, 'Right now all me'n Damon got to sweat about is Sam Crawford an' his Bar SC animals.' Damon and the thin tall man shared an inability to sleep just because it was dark so they put the candle in the middle of the table and played Pedro and were still playing it after the others slept and snored.

It was past midnight when a horse whistled. Damon looked across the table when he asked if the taller man knew of bears, cougars or wolves being in the area. Charley Oden's answer was candidly given. 'Not that I know of. Last year when we made a gather I come on to what was left of an old dry cow. Len said it was bears. You want to go outside?'

Damon was willing, despite the damper being closed down it was uncomfortably hot in the shack. He made a light joke as he arose. 'When I'm losin' I take a walk.'

Charley laughed but not loud enough to awaken the sleepers.

They left the candle burning. They also did not close the door fully. The shack needed cooling. In fact it needed airing.

There was half a moon and it was chilly as they left the house on their way to the corral. Whatever had upset the horses was still in the neighbourhood; they were acting like colts, throwing their heads and snorting. Damon said, 'Go around the far side. I'll go the near side.'

Damon hadn't gone a hundred feet before he thought he saw movement among a stand of lodgepole pines and stopped near an old deadfall and hunkered, six-gun in hand. It was a long wait and darkness did not help as he tried to outline whatever he had seen. He was ready to try sidling northerly until he could flank whatever he had seen, or thought he had seen, when Charley let out a howl that could have been heard at the far side of the meadow.

Damon changed hands with his six-gun in order to wipe off sweat in his gun hand. He sidled as far as the deadfall was long then changed course.

It was a long, slow trail and when he was certain he was behind whatever had spooked him, he used undergrowth to start angling due southward.

The spindly trees where he had originally seen movement were clearly outlined and there was nothing but a slight taste of dust.

He turned back. At the corral the horses were lined up shoulder to shoulder peering in the direction he had taken. They were still upset enough to bob their heads occasionally and to make snorty sounds.

He reached the front of the corral, saw movement dead ahead, faded into darkness until he made out a silhouette and stopped when Charley shakily said, 'You see it, Damon?'

'Saw something north-west but never got close. Why'd you holler?'

'Damon, you believe in ghosts?'

'I don't know. I've never seen one. Is that why you yelled? Charley, come out where I can see you.'

Charley moved slightly and halted. 'Squatty feller, thick built. He didn't even make a sound. Can you see past me?'

Damon leaned to his left and to his right. 'All I can see is you, an' can't see you real well. You sure, Charley? What was he doing?'

'Aim, Damon, I'm goin' to walk toward you. If he follers, shoot.'

Damon wiped his palm again before raising his six-gun. He had no intention of shooting; the only movement made was made by the tall rangeman.

When they were together Charley

looked back and his gun hand was unsteady. He said, 'Let's get inside.'

The candle was still burning, it brightened the entire inside of the cabin, not glowingly but adequately. Charley went to a bench and dropped down. He did not holster his handgun until Damon told him to.

Damon fished forth his tobacco plug and offered it. Charley shook his head. He smoked, he did not chew. Damon did both. He gnawed off a cud and cheeked it before he said, 'What was it? Did you see it?'

Charley's eyes widened on Damon. 'I seen it. I damn near walked right into it. Liked to scairt hell out of me.'

'Did it come for you?'

'I don't know. It didn't make any noise. I think it was fixin' to jump me.'

'Why didn't you shoot it?' Damon asked.

'I couldn't hardly move . . . I quit. When Crawford comes up tomorrow he can pay me off.'

Damon went to expectorate in the

stove. When he returned Charley had fisted his six-gun, aiming it steadily at the door.

Damon recalled his own experience but now, later, he wasn't sure he had seen anything.

He watched Charley roll into two blankets on the floor facing the door with his six-gun in his right hand.

He didn't own a watch and had no idea of the time but thought it was late. He stoked the stove, found an old moth-eaten tan army blanket and bedded down near the stove. He did not sleep well. All his life he'd been a hard sleeper but not this night.

When he awakened he was alone in the cabin. It only required minutes for him to get ready for the new day; he went outside. It was still dark and the moon was far toward the horizon as if to make way for the sun. The horses had been fed and acted normally. There was no sound of the other men until someone made a booming sound easterly. Damon would know that voice as long as he lived. He saw Marshal Kimball working his way past stands of spindly pine and fir trees.

Damon waited, leaning on the topmost corral stringer. When Kimball saw him he began wagging his head. When they were closer he said, 'That's the gawddamnest thing I ever saw.' Damon followed the marshal into the cabin. Kimball stood with his back to the stove eyeing his companion. 'I've seen 'em scairt peeless but never like that feller.'

Damon went to a bench. 'Where's them other two?'

'Still out there,' Kimball retorted in a voice that echoed with disgust. 'You didn't go over there?'

Damon shook his head. 'The horses got skittish in the night so I took Charley to scout around. I went west. He went east.'

'Then you didn't see it?'

'See what?'

'What Charley saw.'

'Walt! Damn it!'

The older man had avoided looking straight at Damon. He did now as he said, 'You ever see a mummy, boy?'

Damon arose looking irritable. 'Where is it!'

'East, boy. Go east maybe short of a half-mile. Maybe a little more'n a quarter-mile. In a little clearing.'

Damon left the cabin, was freeing-up the tie-down thong over his sidearm when he nearly collided with the other two men.

Pete stared. 'No one out here, Damon. We poked around . . . '

'See for myself,' Damon replied annoyedly and pushed past. They faced around to watch his progress easterly for a few moments then went inside and slammed the old door after themselves.

For Damon the puny moonlight was a little better than no light at all as he ducked around and past a number of growing saplings, side-stepping thick upthrusts of brutish growth, some of it with stickers.

There was a clearing ahead. He set his course by the amount of unobstructed moonlight that touched there.

It was a longer hike than he had anticipated. Once he paused to grope for his plug and worry off a man-sized chew. As he was standing amid the spindly trees something on his left, which was north, gave a great jump and lit down running. He growled around his cud. 'Damn deer. Maybe a worth-while buck, but I'm not huntin'. Well, not deer huntin'.'

As he pushed ahead a soft ankle-high little breeze swept toward him from the clearing. He didn't stop but he picked his way with more caution. The area hereabouts was stiff with the stumps of those spindly trees. By daylight he would have divined the reason but in this degree of shadowy night it was not possible to detect any pattern to the way the trees had been downed.

At the same moment a cougar squawled not too far off, he saw it.

The marshal was right. The base was

semi-square with rounded corners and was made of mortared stones. Above it was what remained of a Sioux burial platform. Atop it was what was left of the mummy bundle, only this one wasn't lying flat out as customary. With this one the arms were folded on the chest and the head was looking forward. The dead man, what remained after birds and small climbing varmints had finished with it, was fixed in a sitting position. A considerable amount of flesh remained in strips, the thick mane of jet-black hair was pretty much as it had been in life, but the face had shrivelled features about half picked clean to the bone and — unusual — the eyes had not been picked out. They looked straight ahead.

The old bronco had a rifle across his lap. Its wooden parts had been decorated with crude carving and studded designs made noticeable because of the way little brass tacks were arranged.

Damon did not move. Small animals

in nearby underbrush thickets made rattling sounds as they burrowed deeper in their haste to go elsewhere.

A large bird as black as a crow lofted himself into the air from behind the sitting corpse and let go with an unnerving squawk as it disappeared eastward. He — it — had evidently spent the night roosting with the dead Indian, behind him.

Damon's legs turned loose under him. He sat down holding the six-gun in his right hand in his lap.

Because it was customary to talk, Damon addressed the long-dead Indian. 'How long you been up there? Aren't no Indians in this part of the country I've heard of in forty, fifty years? How's come they left the rifle with you? They prized them real high. Who in hell are you . . . *who was you?*'

In a frightening situation the sound of a voice helps the recovery from shock, even if it's the only voice.

The answer Damon got nearly stopped his heart. That cougar screamed again.

Damon squirmed where he sat, got twisted around and jack-knifed up to his feet. He remembered the pistol and hung fire long enough to holster it.

The hike back was interrupted by several halts for Damon to look back and elsewhere before continuing his march in the direction of the old cabin.

When he walked in the others were eating at the table. They waited until he'd closed the door before resuming eating. The only one to speak was the tallest of them. Charley spoke around a mouthful of food. 'Did he talk to you, Damon?'

Pete went to the stove, filled a plate and returned to point with greasy fingers as he said, 'Eat, young 'un.'

Damon went instead to the stove, stood with his back to it and finally spoke. 'If that there is a joke it's sure a sickenin' one.'

Pete took it up. The others continued to be busy eating. Dawn light was seeping past the cracks in the walls.

Damon said, 'Marshal, you been

around here the longest . . . '

Walt Kimball was wiping his hands on a faded old bandanna.

'I've heard, boy. Every place I ever been I've heard about them things but I haven't come face to face with any of 'em. Sit down'n eat, boy. That coffee's hot, that's about all I can say for it.'

Pete Forchay stopped chewing long enough to put a sulphurous glare in the lawman's direction.

Damon did not eat. He did not leave his place by the stove until they all heard men shouting from the south.

Charley stood up and left the table. 'That'll be Sam an' maybe Len. I'll go look after their horses.'

After the tall man departed, Walt sourly said, 'Rush out'n polish the boss's boots. I've known 'em like that before.'

The men outside were out there a long time. They did not follow Charley into the cabin until Pete and the others had just about finished cleaning up after the meal.

Walt Kimball knew the large old man and the lithe, weathered man who had made the ride with him, Leonard Holt. After hands had been shaken, Sam Crawford said he knew about the Indian burial platform.

Pete Forchay stoked the stove, stirred hash and poured coffee. Pete had hired on as a rangeman but he'd demonstrated a rare talent for cooking and, when they got back to the home place, he would do precious little cowboying; it was a waste of his talent. Every big cow outfit needed a good cook; that was one of the reasons riders hired on and stayed on.

Charley and Damon said they would go out and saddle horses. Sam and his range boss wanted to look at the cattle. Before they left the cabin Sam told the rangemen to sit down and get comfortable, he had a story to tell them.

There was little doubt about the story among the riders. Getting comfortable wasn't difficult for men who spent a good part of their days straddling leather.

Sam refilled his own cup at the stove, returned to the table, set the cup aside and said, 'For me it was the toss of a coin whether you'd stumble on to that old burial site. Well, there's a few old-timers who knew about it an' by now they're mostly dead. This is good coffee, Pete.'

'Thanks, Mr Crawford.'

The rugged old cowman got as comfortable on a bench at the table as it was possible to get. He avoided looking directly at anyone. 'This was before any of you was born . . . things was different. It was before I got married . . . It was some time before my wife died . . . ' Crawford looked up. He was wearing some kind of smile. It could have been apologetic or just plain uncomfortable but stories about the upland Crawford range had been told and retold and not once had it been related in a manner that did credit to old Sam Crawford.

'There was Indians a-plenty when I come to this country. Soldiers chased 'em, fought 'em, corralled some an' took them away in cattle cars . . . they're gone.' Crawford flicked a glance at his range boss who was occupied cleaning his boots with a pocket knife.

Sam continued, 'It's dang near impossible to run cattle where there's Indians, but I done it, took my losses and kept back replacement heifers. It was hard work an' a long haul.

'Now'n then we'd catch a few running off my cattle. There was fights . . . plenty of fights until the army come in force, made a big gather an' things got better.' Crawford was quiet for a rather lengthy period of time before he spoke again.

'Well, they wasn't all thievin' bastards. The army didn't draw no line. They come in wagons for them as didn't have horses. It was a sorry time, boys. I'd got pretty close with some of 'em.'

The range boss stopped cleaning his boots and looked at Crawford. The old man cleared his throat. 'Now then, that burial place. The Indian was big among them. His name don't matter . . . that's him over yonder. Underneath the rock slab is another grave, the old man's daughter. I was down in Texas buyin' cattle.' Crawford went to refill his cup at the stove. He returned to the table, tasted the coffee and pushed the cup away. His range boss went to also refill his cup. He and the old man exchanged a look as the range boss went back to his place and sat down. Sam Crawford went to open the door as wide as it would go and returned to the table. 'The soldiers took 'em all away . . . to a reservation the old man told me. His daughter died down there. He brought her back in a bundle. It's her underneath the old man. He chose the spot; they had a camp there, quite a bunch of 'em. I helped him. I was still young then, he was old. He drew me a picture how he wanted to be buried

. . . how he wanted to be lookin' westerly.' The old man looked at Charley. 'Scairt you, did it?'

'Scairt the hell out of me, Mr Crawford. Didn't the Indian want to be buried in the ground like his daughter?'

'No. I still got the picture he made, an' we both worked over there right up until he died.' Sam looked at the marshal before he resumed. 'Then I finished it alone; exactly the way he wanted it to be.'

The old man arose looking directly ahead and walked out of the cabin. The coffee pot was empty. Pete went about making a fresh pot. He was the only one who had moved after Sam Crawford had left the house.

The range boss took his cup of java and went to stand in the doorway. The thin man asked Leonard a question. 'You know anythin' about this?'

The range boss turned slowly. 'Yes. If Sam comes back tell him I've gone to sift through the cattle.'

Walt nodded. The range boss passed

from sight and Pete Forchay said, 'If it's his secret he didn't have to explain it to us.'

Walt nodded curtly. 'He'd have had a reason, wouldn't he?'

Damon went to the door as though he too meant to leave the cabin. He jerked straight up and froze a couple of feet beyond the doorway. He turned slowly and addressed the marshal when he said, 'You better come look, Marshal.'

There were three of them with carbines across their laps. They were herding the range boss toward the cabin. His holster was empty and his expression was set in stone.

Where they reined up in front of the cabin Sam Crawford appeared leading his saddle animal. He too was expressionless until Leonard said, 'Dogged us, Walt.'

One of the three newcomers urged his mount closer and faced Sam. 'You didn't include these critters, Mr Crawford.'

Sam responded brusquely 'But you found 'em, Mr Lincoln.'

Whoever Lincoln was he said, 'They was erased off'n the inventory. Mind tellin' me why? You aren't stealin' your own cattle, are you?'

Sam ignored the question when he said, 'Get down, gents. Coffee's in the house.'

5

A Long Night

The pair of riders accompanying the younger man would never be mistaken for anything but rangemen from their silver-mounted spurs to their horsehair hatbands. One man looked older than his friends who were not only fairly young but both were dark enough to be Indians, except that they were Mexicans. One was named Rubio Estevan, but even if folks hadn't heard the name his spurs, and other silver-inlaid articles, his six-gun, his big Chihuahua spurs also heavily overlaid and engraved, were either of Mexican or South Texas origin. His friend was named Enrico Gomez.

He sat his saddle behind the rider who had spoken, studying the marshal, the other men who were either in the yard or were emerging from the cabin. He said something in Mex-Spanish to the men facing Sam Crawford and Marshal Kimball.

The man he had addressed replied curtly in English. 'It had to be them. A blind man could read those tracks.' The speaker looked at Walt as he swung from the saddle to the ground. 'Anythin' else besides coffee, Mr Crawford? Real food? We been in the saddle since yestiddy.'

Pete Forchay spoke from the doorway. 'Mulligan an' cobbler made from wild apples.'

The strangers dismounted looking pleased.

The man who was apparently the head of the newcomers clearly had a fondness for apple pie. He smiled at Pete. 'Wild apples you say?'

Forchay handled the situation better than Sam had. He said, 'Tie up, boys, 'n come inside.'

Sam Crawford took Walt aside. 'It's a long story . . . I sold that one — his name's Harry Lincoln — two hunnert head, mostly young stock . . . '

'An' you drove some of his two hunnert up here?'

'Well, I didn't include these critters. I've been workin' on them for some years, tryin' to raise up a breed of belted animals; I called 'em Crawford's Belted Best.'

Marshal Kimball regarded his companion closely. 'An' you held these back?'

'Walt, every one of those heifers is bred to a belted bull. You understand?'

'No. Not if you sold them to this feller. What'd you say his name was?'

'Harry Lincoln.'

The lawman's eyes widened. 'Related to . . . ?'

'No! That's the first thing he makes plain. Abe Lincoln was no relation to any of his family. Walt, he's a south Texan. They was Rebels an' had nothin' to do with Lincoln's Northerners.'

'Well, can't say I'm sorry to hear that. I warn't a Union man myself. You sold him these cattle?'

'I didn't mean to, Walt. I sold him by count not by markings.'

'Was you hidin' these critters?'

'Well, not exactly. I just never intended for Lincoln to get this bunch. It's only a few head.'

'I get the feelin' he don't know that.'

Pete poked his head past the door. 'Food's on,' he yelled and ducked back inside.

It was a unique meal. There was very little conversation until later when, as was customary, the men went outside to enjoy a smoke. Damon told the marshal that the range boss for some reason stayed pretty much by himself. 'Except for Sam Crawford,' he said. The range boss seemed to avoid the others, which wasn't exactly accurate. Len, the range boss, and the tall rider called Charley, got along very well. Kimball's rejoinder to that was a few words followed by a scornful grunt.

'They both work for Sam Crawford. Far as I know they have for some years.

A man can't work alongside another feller for any length of time an' neither chum up with him nor avoid him like the mumps.'

Sam and the younger cattleman named Lincoln went out by the corral. When their absence was noticed, Crawford's range boss also left the cabin. Damon told the marshal he would go pitch feed to the horses and Walt caught him by the shirt wagging his head. 'Stay here,' he told Damon. 'Leave them be out yonder. They got business to discuss.'

Evidently that is what happened because when Sam returned to the cabin he told the others he wanted the cattle bunched.

That's all he told them. As they trooped out to the corrals, Harry Lincoln was already astride and with his riders. Between Damon and Walt the conversation was brief. Damon asked the marshal why they should help in someone else's roundup. Kimball's reply was quietly given. 'I'd guess that if they're gathered today, it'll make it easy for one of those gents to drive 'em. You can wait here if you're of a mind.'

Damon rigged out his animal. When the marshal shoved his left boot into the stirrup to mount up Damon did the same.

The day wasn't going to last much longer. The sun was already off centre. As the riders headed out Walt told Damon making the gather and driving them to Crawford's yard hadn't ought to take long, but he was wrong.

There was a fair-sized crew spreading out on the meadow, riding at a walk. Roundups were not made at a dead run. If riders bust out in a dead run cattle would scatter to Kingdom Come and some would never be seen again.

Walt and Damon rode wide northward and did not begin to close in until the cattle were walking toward each other. At a dead walk it required no more than half an hour to get the animals bunched. Harry Lincoln and his *vaqueros* had the lead; they led the herd toward the best place for them to bed down, and stopped. The other riders came in from the sides until the bunching was completed, then they stopped riding.

The cattle began to graze, they drifted a little in order to find feed and the riders allowed them to do that, but not far. They held their loose circle until the sun was teetering on mountain tops, then they worked around until they met. Sam and Charley dismounted. Harry Lincoln joined them. They sat on the ground until the sun was gone before mounting as the cattle sought a satisfactory bedding ground, folded their legs beneath them, got plumb down and were bedded. They would be in those places until first light, and then the drive would begin down out of Shipman's Meadow.

Sam Crawford led off on the return ride to the cabin. He and his range boss rode side by side without fifteen words passing between them until the house was in sight. Then Crawford dropped back to ride with Harry Lincoln.

Sam did most of the talking; most of the explaining. For years he had considered starting a new variety of belted cattle. He had very carefully held back only the largest, best-boned heifers. Thus far he hadn't had much success with belted bulls but he was working on it. One of these days . . . he would wait if it took the rest of his life. Not just one belted bull, several of them to breed back to his belted cows. Lincoln slouched along in silence. He had been a long time in the saddle.

He was dog tired but not so tired he didn't think about what he had done when he bought all those Crawford animals. He could pick it up where Sam Crawford would have to give it up. He was a good twenty years younger than Sam Crawford; by the time they were off-saddling at the cabin he had pretty well worked it out in his mind: Lincoln's Oversized Purebred Belted Cattle!

Lincoln ate supper apart and afterwards went out into the night to do some pondering. He hadn't just bought those Crawford cattle, he had also bought the old man's dream. Somewhere down the road he would be the sole source of extra large, big-boned belted cows by the hundreds.

He was still out there when Sam Crawford's range boss came out, settled against an adjoining corral stringer of roughly draw-knifed corral poles and said, 'Them's good cattle you bought, Mr Lincoln.'

Since that was obvious it required no verbal confirmation. Lincoln nodded without speaking.

Len took his time building a cigarette. He lighted it and got a head of smoke rising before he spoke again. 'The old man's been up-breedin' an' cross-breedin' that bunch for some time until he got what he wanted.'

Again Lincoln nodded but this time he spoke. 'Size, Leonard. That's what took my eye. They got more size to 'em than anythin' I've seen in a 'coon's age.'

This time it was the range boss who nodded. He also said, 'For a while, until them belted cattle are spread around, you won't have to brand. Not only that, Mr Lincoln, but you can identify them cattle as far as you can see. For a while anyway brandin' irons'll just hang on the wall. You got any idea how long Sam's been breedin' up the size an' markin' he wanted? Six, eight years . . . he let everythin' else go, until he got down to where he had to sell some critters. You made a good buy, Mr Lincoln.'

Harry Lincoln neither agreed nor disagreed, he went back to the cabin.

The range boss lingered. Eventually he worked his way easterly and had another smoke sitting on the mortared base of that old tomb or whatever it was. But this time he removed his hat and let it fall beside him.

It was one of those nights where a man could hear a pin drop at twenty feet.

He was bone tired. He leaned back, stubbed out the smoke and was awakened roughly by someone's big work-calloused hand shaking him by the shoulder. The range boss looked up as Sam Crawford said, 'I figured you'd be over here. Come along, Len, the others is bedded down at the cabin. You'll catch your death of the grippe settin' out here when the night turns cold. Get up, Len. Let's go back.'

They went back, walked the full distance without a word passing between them.

A candle was still burning, sleeping men snorted and snored in the semi-gloom and because the last man to roll in had stoked the fire the cabin was still warm. Too warm for blankets. That would change before dawn.

Sam Crawford was asleep almost before he got sprawled on the floor under one old blanket someone had left folded on the table beside another folded blanket.

His range boss didn't sleep well. He

might have later in the night; he'd put in a long, hard day, but he was still lying there looking straight up when he heard a critter bawl.

Any man born and raised among cattle detected sound and could place it in his sleep. It came again, a different pitch this time from roughly the same direction, south-westerly.

Len looked over. Sam was sleeping the sleep of the dead. Len did not awaken him. He arose, stamped into his boots, went to the doorway, stood in the opening breathing deeply of fresh night air as a number of cattle with differently pitched voices bawled. It wasn't the sound of frightened animals, it was the bawling of animals on the move.

Len went back, leaned over Sam and stirred him awake.

Sam sat up with his mouth hanging open. He looked up to say something and the bawling, fainter but unmistakable, sounded. Len said, 'They're bein' drove. I'll bet you my life on it.'

Sam rolled out feeling for his boots

as he said, 'Wake the others, Len.' He stood up to pick up his shellbelt and make certain the old Colt was in its holster.

Len went around using his boot-toe to roust up the others. There was grumbling, profanity and abrupt silence among the men in the cabin who were frozen in place as they listened to bawling cattle. Harry Lincoln came up off the floor like a catamount. 'Sons of bitches!' he said. 'Shut up an' listen!'

They stopped making noise but listened only until they were satisfied, then started for the door. The last man out was Sam Crawford. He blew out the candle.

Rigging out drowsy horses where huge old trees muzzled about half the light, even by men who had been saddling animals most of their lives, was a frustrating experience but they got it done and followed Harry Lincoln away from the cabin clearing, still saying very little, making certain their weapons were loaded.

Charley thought it was wolves. So did Pete Forchay but neither Sam nor the others were convinced; for one thing the bawling was being made by disgruntled animals on the move. If it had been an attack by wolves the bawling would have been coming from different directions. Cattle under attack by wolves fled in panic; they didn't stay bunched.

Sam Crawford caught up with Harry Lincoln. They shared their suspicion. It was Sam who changed direction a tad. He told the younger man they should try to head off the cattle, not just ride behind them.

Damon came up on the near side of Sam and called to him. 'Charley'n I'll make a run ahead. Maybe turn 'em back or stop 'em.'

Whatever Crawford thought of that notion was lost to the pair of younger men as they spurred more easterly, but since this was what Sam'd had in mind, he let them go without speaking.

Where the moon shone across the

meadow the noise of moving cattle provided a fair scent of dust but as yet none of the pursuers had a sighting. Whoever was attempting to steal the cattle kept them moving. Damon thought except for the noise of upset beef whoever was driving them would have no idea they had horsemen coming after them further back.

But that idea didn't last for Damon and Charley, the lanky cowboy. They had pushed their saddle animals hard to cover the distance it was necessary to cover for them to make out moving shadows.

The rustlers' intention seemed to be to push the cattle in the direction of the nearest rank of big trees. The other three directions were more distant. Whether the thieves meant to go west, or whether they were heading in that direction to follow cattle, was anyone's guess but scrawny Charley was covering the distance better than Damon, when up ahead a gunshot sounded from a direction where the cattle only had to cover another quarter-mile to be in among the trees.

After that gunshot Charley slackened his speed until he and Damon were almost riding stirrup but with a fair distance between them.

Damon raised his pistol. He had hoped very hard that the cow-thieves had no idea they were being chased, but after that single gunshot that illusion was destroyed. Nevertheless when Damon could make Charley out in the night, the tall, thin man was riding slightly bent over; more bent over in fact than a man would normally sit a saddle.

Damon alternately watched the cattle and the bouncing silhouette he would have wagered good money was one of the rustlers.

From the south came the sound of three gunshots too close together to be anything but fired from the same gun.

Damon hauled back. Whoever had shot his gun half empty was south and east. Damon abandoned his head-long pursuit, rode instead in the direction of the tall man. When he had covered half the distance he could see Charley bending lower until he fell off his horse. Damon swore! Charley had been hit!

Whoever was south and east was in the best position to cut in front of the cattle before they reached the trees.

Damon's horse was bewildered. With his rider preparing to dismount he slackened off until he slowed to a clumsy trot.

When enough distance had been closed, Damon left his horse in a leap, kicked through a wiry stand of undergrowth and almost fell over Charley who was leaning into a thicket; half sitting, half standing, supported by the thicket. Charley slowly turned his head.

Damon saw the blood before he got close enough to kneel and push brush aside. Charley was looking straight at him. He said, 'Lost my damned horse . . . which one are you?'

'Damon. Hold still.'

Bullets had hit a lot of men, but very

rarely the way Charley had been hit. There was blood on his shoulder, it had run down his left sleeve. Where Charley's hat had been there was a gash halfway around his head above the ears.

Damon's visibility was poor because of the huge old trees and flourishing stands of brush. He touched the wound. Charley didn't move. Damon knew nothing about head wounds, wounds in general, but one thing was obvious, the bleeding had to be stopped.

He talked as he cut the sleeve from Charley's shirt on the far side and continued to talk as he fashioned a bandage that did not stop the bleeding but stanched the worst of it.

Charley seemed to feel very little. As Damon talked, Charley began answering him, but Charley's conversation had nothing to do with where he was, why he was there, or even who Damon was and what Damon was doing to Charley's wound.

Both of them were mottled with

blood but very little was seeping from beneath the bandage. Damon reared back on his heels and said, 'Partner, you're out of it. I guess I am too, Charley . . . ?'

'Yeah? What?'

'Can you understand what we been talkin' on about?'

Charley's reply came clearly. 'Yeah, one of those rustlin' bastards shot at me.'

'He hit you, Charley. I'll get your horse. Can you set the saddle?'

'I can ride if that's what you mean. Why?'

'Because I'll boost you into the saddle an' you head south.'

'They went west, Damon, not south.'

'Never mind about them, Charley. You ride south, back the way you come up here. Hold on to the nubbin with both hands an' keep goin' south until you find some people. You understand?'

Charley scrabbled in the thicket to arise. He paused long enough to say, 'I understand . . . keep goin' toward the

101

settlement until I come on to someone that'll help.'

Damon leaned to see how much blood was running, tightened the bandage and left Charley long enough to find his horse.

He found the animal. It was standing with Damon's horse — and a third horse with Pete Forchay holding the reins.

Damon told Pete about Charley, took the reins of his animal and the one Charley had ridden, and explained to Pete where Charley was, why he was there, and told Pete to take Charley southward to the first set of buildings he found and get him taken care of.

Pete helped boost the tall Texan into the saddle, took the reins and headed down-country. Damon called after him, 'Watch him; he'll likely fall off.'

Pete did not respond, he led Charley's horse in a southward sashay. Damon watched until he was satisfied they would make it before mounting up. He did not believe he would find the rustlers or the stolen cattle, but he had to make the effort.

With no idea how long he'd spent with Charley and unable to hear any sounds of ridden horses or driven cattle, he poked along listening.

That portion of the moon which had shown was no longer in sight and the night was getting colder.

Between the forest on Damon's right and no moon it was impossible to see movement until a belted bull came out of the timber in a lumbering westward run. Damon was reining to get behind the bull when a *vaquero* got on his opposite side, evidently without seeing Damon, and raced ahead to turn the bull back. In the murky gloom he mistook Damon for one of his companions and yelled in Spanish to help reverse the bull's course.

Damon stopped stone still and drew his six-gun. Another rider appeared to Damon's left. He was less than a yard away when he pulled his horse to an abrupt, sliding halt. He started to yell when he saw the fisted six-gun in

Damon's hand. The *vaquero* apparently did not see the newcomer; he continued to spur toward overtaking the man chasing the bull, but the newcomer not only was close enough to see Damon, he also saw the six-gun aimed in his direction.

Damon ignored the bull and the *vaquero* to yell for the newcomer to drop his weapon and dismount. The man swung to the ground with one rein in his hand. Damon reined in his direction as he yelled, 'The gun! Drop it!'

Damon's adversary was a *gringo*; he immediately disarmed himself and stood stone still as Damon reined ahead, leaned from the saddle to unbuckle the horse's throat latch and make an overhand strike with the bridle that stung the horse on the rump. It threw up its head to yank at the freed reins and ran southward past Damon, across the clearing where the bull and his pursuer had gone and lunged wildly among the trees where it was lost to sight in moments.

6

A Long Night Ends

Damon sat his horse eyeing his prisoner. He was a *gringo* not tall nor heavy and perfectly willing to stand without moving. Damon said, 'You got a belly gun?' When the stranger shook his head Damon asked the man his name and got a prompt reply.

'Goodwin. Texas Goodwin an' no, I don't pack a hideout weapon.'

Before any additional discussion could ensue, several gunshots and some bawling of cattle were accompanied by someone's voice raised in unsteady profanity.

A horseman pushing hard came south. His appearance was both wild-eyed and surprised. Seeing Damon and his prisoner the man yelled in Spanish for Damon's prisoner to go back the way he had come and run for it.

Damon's captive spun to face the rider and yelled to him, 'Russ! Give it up!'

Damon watched his second captive haul back to a sliding halt and yelled at the man to disarm himself. It was good advice. What made it exceptionally good was when Damon shifted his pistol barrel a fraction and said, 'Do it, you son of a bitch.'

The intruder wasted a long moment eyeing Damon before he emptied his holster. The six-gun struck a large rock as it landed and its disarmed owner made a bleating sound as he raised both arms.

A gravelly voice sounded off to the right where the trees were thick. 'Boy, I don't know how you did it.'

Sam Crawford worked his way until he was fully in sight then drew rein, let one hand rest on the saddle swells while he rummaged for a pretty badly mauled plug of Mule Shoe. As he bit off a cud he studied the strangers, leaned to expectorate and said,

'The critters'll be along directly. They fetched up against a big *barranca*. There's no way to go around it so they turned and charged back. Len's got one of them rustlers.'

One of the captives shook his head, swore a blue streak before addressing the old man.

'I never in my life worked as hard for nothin' as I done tonight.'

Sam worked his cud from one cheek to the other, took his time, and eventually asked a question.

'Mister, who do you ride for?'

The disgusted man gave the old man look for look when he answered. 'Mister, I don't think you'd know him. The four of us work for Sheriff Cutler of Sioux County up north.'

Sam accepted that. 'I know him. By reputation anyway. He's been sellin' stolen cattle up over the border into Canada for longer'n you are old. What's your name?'

'Russell Thomas ... yours is Sam Crawford?'

The old man nodded as the sound of panicky cattle got closer.

Harry Lincoln with two men sashayed their way into sight; that unreliable moon was peeping over the top of an immense half mountain of which the other half was the far side of that blockading mountain called a *barranca*. The gap between was at least 200 feet straight down.

Another *vaquero* walked his horse in the direction of the voices. When he saw the other *vaquero* his unhappy expression changed. He called ahead in Spanish and only stopped when the other Mexican told him to come ahead with both hands in sight.

The old man asked about Pete and Charley and Damon told him; Forchay had taken Charley to find aid for a wound Charley had incurred.

One of the captives was a chewer. He was handed a plug and settled into a silence that matched the taciturnity of the other captives.

Bawling cattle were a short mile back

in the direction from which they had come, still bawling to match the shouts of the men who were driving them.

The moon was gone, the bitter cold of predawn was in place and by count about half the cattle trooped tiredly past, head hung and bleary-eyed. They paid no attention to the motionless riders. Sam told the men to scatter and find the missing cattle. As the riders moved to obey, Sam told Damon to stay with him. Stray critters bawled, lost in the timber and seeking companions. It would not be difficult to place them, make a loose gather and drive.

Sam got a fresh cut cheeked. They had three prisoners which meant there was still one more or maybe a pair somewhere, possibly lost in the forests.

It didn't matter. Sam asked questions of the captives they were riding with and got all the information he needed, plus something that surprised him. It appeared that the wholesale rustling lawman up north had heard of the belted cattle and had sent his hirelings to find them and drive them north.

Len smiled. 'If he peddled them over the line sure as hell someone might have heard of them and scouted them up out of curiosity.'

The difficulty to that, Damon suggested, was if that up-north lawman rustler had a reduction works to sell the cattle to, by the time anyone from down south could do the necessary tracking the critters would have been reduced to ground meat. If Sam's special cattle got cut up whether he could prove anything or not he would have to start his special breeding programme all over again and at his age . . .

Sam straightened up in the saddle and said, 'Son of a bitch!'

Sam had another decision to make, whether to ride to the big meadow, wait and count critters as they dragged in, or head for the high country. In the high country when cold arrived it went through everything a man wore and chilled him to the bone.

They headed for the cabin after Sam

sent his range boss to the meadow.

By the time Damon forked feed to the horses and parceled out what little dusty ground grain he could find, Sam had a fire going and without Pete Forchay to make a meal he parceled the job out to the captive named Thomas to rassle up a hot meal. He had his back to the rustler so he failed to see the look Thomas put on him. Russell Thomas was a top-hand rangeman not a cook.

The cabin warmed up, the men eyed one another without much conversation. Outside, the cold increased despite the sun having arrived.

Sam took Damon out to the corrals and explained what he wanted done about locating any belted cattle up north. He gave Damon all the information he had about the livestock-stealing lawman up north. To make his idea have appeal, old Sam promised Damon a full-time job as one of his ranch hands, plus fifty dollars when he returned — with prisoners or the next best thing.

Damon hung fire. He wanted to stay with the others until they were locked up in someone's jailhouse.

Sam's problem did not include any delay so he upped the ante. 'Damon, seventy-five dollars if you nail them up there an' if you figure some way to come back here with 'em, an even one hunnert dollars.'

It was a temptation that would have appealed powerfully to most raggedy-assed roustabouts, but Damon stalled. He told Sam he never made a decision on an empty stomach and left Crawford where Marshal Kimball found him and helped care for the horses at the corral. The horses were as tucked up as snow birds and caked with drying sweat. The horses went first to tank up on water then put ears back and chased each other away from the feed. Walt Kimball was draping his Navajo saddle blanket sweat-side up to dry when Damon came over to explain Sam Crawford's offer.

The marshal vigorously scratched

while leaning against the corral watching his horse, so his response was not just slow coming but when he spoke he shocked hell out of Damon.

'Boy, you never went after lawbreakers in your life, an' while you're pretty savvy an' all, you go up north by yourself to catch them bastards an' all you'll accomplish is to get yourself killed.'

Damon slowly faced away from the marshal. After a moment of silence he said, 'If you'd come along, you'd have to up'n quit your marshalin' job, an' we might be up there beatin' the bushes for weeks.' Damon turned. 'If he'll match the offer he made me, to you . . . go ask him, Walt. If he'll agree I'll be downright happy. But I don't think he will an' I don't figure to split what he offered me with you.'

The large older man gave Damon look for look before saying, 'Stay right here, boy. I'll be back directly.'

For an individual as hefty and old as Walt Kimball was he could move well with proper motivation, and $100 in a country where most men did not receive that kind of pay for several months' work, Walt possibly established some kind of high-country record in leaving the corral and reaching the shack where someone had proved how cold-blooded he was by putting wood in the stove that was beginning to get cherry red.

Sam was drinking from a canteen, for the third time since getting back when Walt braced him. He lowered the canteen and looked steadily at the marshal. 'What in hell are you talkin' about? That boy's downright coyote; no one's goin' to trip him up.'

Kimball snorted. 'He's a greenhorn, Sam. He never sidled up to a pet dog, an' besides, if we can save them cattle of yours it'll make things up for the lost time.'

'What lost time! Walt, what in — '

'Sam, the lost time if them critters get butchered up north. It'll take you another three years to get other heifers ready to go to the bull. Sam, you don't have that many years left to squander.'

Sam put the two-thirds empty canteen aside before he said, 'Tell you what, Walt, you find my belted critters an' bring 'em back here an' I'll pay you the . . . hunnert dollars.'

'That hunnert's got nothin' to do with the hunnert you promised Damon, does it?'

'No! The pair of you do what you're figurin' to do an' each one of you gets one hunnert dollars.' Sam looked around at the motionless, startled men sweating with him in the too-hot room, and said something else in a lowered tone of voice. 'If you do it . . . as sure as I'm standin' here I'll have a stroke.'

The marshal shot back his answer. 'Sam, you make out your Will an' be sure you put this part in it. Both me'n the lad get one hunnert dollars for completin' things.'

Sam's expression and colouring made it seem he was going to have the stroke as he stood there. That cherry-red stove might have had some reason for the old man to look as he did.

The lawman filled both coat pockets with food, cooked and uncooked, without looking at the others, gave his hat an extra hard pull as he reset it, and stamped out of the house to be face to face with an immense rising sun.

Sam Crawford followed him. Where they met at the corral the lawman said, 'We'll take these cattle to the shipping pens down south an' hold 'em until we get this straightened out. Sam, you can't sell them critters to two buyers at the same time.'

The cowman leaned on the topmost stringer of the corral to watch the horses lipping up the last few stalks. When he faced the marshal he wagged his head.

'Over the years I've babied them belted critters like they was my children.'

'You sold 'em, Sam.'

'I was plumb desperate, Walt. He

won't have to pay for them.'

Marshal Kimball did not look hopeful. 'If he's been lookin' for somethin' special in the livestock line, I'd give odds he won't relinquish 'em back to you. Get hold of yourself. I'm dog-ass tired an' I expect you'n the others are too. But let's take those critters down below an' corral 'em until everything is settled, an' maybe Lincoln won't want to do that. It's some miles south and those lads he hired to drive 'em would go north.'

What the two older men had been discussing required no additional discussion especially when Sam Crawford brushed past on his way back to the cabin leaving the marshal with the only alternative. He followed him.

No one, not even the captives — hired rustlers — would be eager to make a fresh gather and head for the south with it. But when the others finished eating they were ready to get rigged out, get astride and head for the big meadow.

It required an hour to make the gather, the critters did not spook, which might have been expected, they watched for the leaders to begin the down-country hike and dutifully fell in behind. The animals were tired, they'd spent something like half the previous night running or being driven. What little rest they'd had was nowhere nearly as much as they needed. Even passing through forested uplands did not inspire them to do anything but trudge in the wake of their leaders.

Harry Lincoln's riders spoke among themselves in a language the others did not understand. They were satisfied to be going south. If they went south far enough they'd be back where they belonged.

But the other riders either sulked or argued. For them the drive from that big meadow down yonder was almost as much as a drive from the village to Sam Crawford's customary grazing country. They knew little about why they were heading for any corrals and not straight for home.

It did not particularly matter, the horsemen leading off seemed to have reason for leading the critters in the direction they were going.

It had taken something more than a day to reach the uplands, returning down-country required two full days. The animals they were driving were not only weary they were also preponderantly foot sore and did not get clear of rocky territory until the morning of the second day.

By the time the men had the corrals in sight south of the clutch of buildings they had eaten everything they'd brought along and two of Lincoln's *vaqueros* were riding tender-footed horses. One of them explained to Walt Kimball that where they came from men only had to shoe their horses when there was a genuine reason; when a horse got gimpy they turned it out and brought in a fresh one. It was one of those range-country mysteries that was never fully explained, but before the drive had the village in sight its inhabitants knew a small cattle drive was coming.

Some of the drovers favoured bedding down north of town, not trying to corral the critters at sunset or later. It made good sense. They sent a rider ahead to acquire enough of everything required to provide for two meals, went into camp, traded off being night hawks so the cattle wouldn't wander and hunkered around the supper-fire as was customary. The main difference was that while ordinarily drovers talked, teased and joked after eating, this night camp was blessed with almost no talking, even among Harry Lincoln's *vaqueros* — who were not comfortable with English.

Damon and Walt Kimball discussed riding north to find the professional rustlers until Walt kept falling asleep, then they too rolled in.

When Damon awakened in predawn cold he rousted the marshal, who did not take kindly being aroused in the dark but stamped into his boots and helped the younger man get the breakfast-fire going after which Damon suggested they ride into the village.

Marshal Kimball was favourable. They caught their horses and rigged up. No one challenged them as they rode away.

Damon's objective was the corrals south and east of town. Getting the cattle into pens they'd never seen before ensured considerable work and bawling cattle. Maybe the noise was not heard as far as the camp but it surely was among the villagers.

Before they had all the critters corralled there were lights showing among the houses. Whether folks were accustomed to it or not bawling cattle could almost raise the dead.

Whoever had created the corrals did an excellent job except in one thing; instead of a pair of wide twin gates there was only one gate, not wide enough when critters crowded to get through.

By the time they had that annoyance cared for everyone within shotgun distance was up and stirring. The fragrance of breakfast stoves at work carried easily to the distant cow camp where men came alive ready to herd critters the last leg of the drive and there were no cattle requiring it.

Several younger villagers came running, stuffing in their shirttails as they ran.

By the time those villagers reached the area the cattle had already been corralled, which did not prevent the aroused village youngsters from making enough of a racket to keep the penned animals from settling down.

Damon went searching for Crawford or Lincoln. As near as he came to success was when Pete Forchay appeared to tell Damon he'd got Charley settled at the distant shack of some settlers who solemnly swore they would care for the wounded man.

Damon's search for Sam, Lincoln, or even Len, the range boss, ended among the business places with the store owners. None of them had seen or spoken to the brace of drovers he was searching for.

Damon was an individual who did not abandon a search. What he found was a freighter with a camp west of the village who had met two riders, one older, one younger man who had a Texan way of talking. They had stopped with him long enough for a cup of hot coffee and had ridden off right after. Their direction according to the freighter had been easterly.

Damon was not an excellent sign reader but with a hot brilliant sun steadily climbing he did not have to be. Two sets of horse tracks led in the only direction two horsemen had gone.

At the moment it did not particularly matter that Damon was a valid tracker. The sign he had been following was made by horses, the animals belonging to the freighter were big mules. Not even the rankest greenhorn that ever came down the line didn't know the difference between horse and mule tracks.

7

An Old Dead Man

Damon's search culminated in defeat. He encountered people who accepted his descriptions as those of men they'd seen but he rode himself ragged without finding whoever he sought.

The day was waning when he left off manhunting and braced Walter Kimball at the hen-house-sized *calabozo*.

Walt had eaten. He had recovered his strength and might have been prepared to sleep. He ignored the clock behind his desk but Damon's sudden and weary appearance stirred him to new life.

He agreed that it made no sense for the owners or pseudo-owners of those cattle to have just plain disappeared.

After Damon provided the marshal with a full itinerary of his manhunt

Kimball slouched at his table, got a decent head of smoke rising and said, 'I don't know, boy. I went around lookin' for at least old Crawford.'

What specifically troubled Damon was that after all he and others had gone through with those damned cattle, whoever-in-hell now owned them should be hanging close, especially old Sam.

The marshal brewed black java on his improvised stove. Damon's hunger was slackened with the coffee but his hunger remained. Walt told him to go somewhere and bed down; in the morning they'd organize a real man-hunt and find the missing men.

It was sound advice except that those corralled animals hadn't been fed since yesterday. The marshal's comment about that was about what Damon might have expected. 'Boy . . . there's not a livin' head of animals that haven't missed a meal or two.'

Damon's alternative was down to nothing when he left Walt Kimball. As this day wore away he went on foot back to the site where the crew he had been riding with had last seen them together, and found Pete Forchay coaxing a supper fire to life. He saw Pete first because of the little fire. Moments after he'd settled in, other men arrived in the gathering darkness. Damon asked questions and got the same answers. None of the men around Pete's fire had seen the others since morning. While Pete served up a passable supper the conversation centred around the missing head men. It was suggested that the missing men might have gone out to Sam's ranch. That idea made no sense. Stockmen didn't just up and abandon their working crews, even if some of them were certainly outlaws.

One of the Texas *vaqueros* stated it as his idea that the other *vaquero*, who was related to him, would never have upped and ridden off, abandoning his cousin.

The discussion was not only lengthy

but the longer it went on the less sense it made. One of the men by the fire rolled into his bedroll and established a precedent the others followed at intervals of disgusted irritability.

Damon was the last to roll in. He was also the first to poke among coals to stir the fire to life the following day when it was as dark as the inside of a well and whoever it was who snored drowned out whatever minimal sounds Damon made before he left the camp at a walk, went around to the marshal's diggings and rousted him up.

As had happened before when the marshal was awakened he did not appreciate being rousted. As he listened to what the younger man had to say he seemed to become less and less enthusiastic. It hadn't made sense the previous night and it made the same amount of sense in the cold darkness of predawn and if he and Damon hadn't had a bond of sorts he would have run off the younger man.

As it was, Walt was fully awakened.

He was hungry, needed a smoke and while pulling on his boots decided a renewed search without half the village spying on them was a good idea. He would ride with the village roustabout.

He grumbled as they left the village by the westerly alleyway with Damon listening without making an attempt to keep the conversation alive. It was dark and cold, there were varmints in the night to be heard but not seen.

Walt finally fell back on his forage rations; a flat tin of oily sardines, the rangeman's last resort. They were rarely liked or enjoyed but a man could carry several of the flat tins and drinking the oil dulled thirst.

The countryside was empty, dark and cold. Neither rider commented on what both had accepted many times but with some of the pleats out of the marshal's stomach, Walt delivered himself of a prodigious belch and spoke.

'Boy, we're not goin' to find 'em out here. You said you wore the subject out last night at Forchay's fire.'

Damon had no answer. He poked along straining to see lights far ahead. The marshal was prepared to add more growling to his remark when his horse, a large, massively muscled bay got the bit between his grinders and shied. He did not simply sidle or snort and sidle, he dropped his head and sprang sideways with more power than he'd demonstrated in years.

His moment of wild panic created a moment of wild gyrations by Damon's mount.

Walt barely avoided going off. He fought the bit without success until Damon's horse came down hard and stayed down.

Marshal Kimball swore a blue streak, fought the horse to a quaking halt, twisted in the saddle and looked back.

He said, 'Gawd'mighty!'

Damon had less trouble. He also fought his mount around. What he saw kept him mute.

The lawman was on the ground with one rein when he spoke again. 'Sam!

Boy, get down here. Help me roll him over.'

Damon obeyed. They both straightened up speechless and staring.

Walt used a boot toe to roll the old cowman onto his back. He did not touch the dead man except to lean and yank off the hat that was crushed down over Sam's face and part of his head.

There was blood, mostly around the head and inside the hat.

Damon turned away then turned back. He used his left foot to roll a large and heavy round rock.

The marshal expelled a long, rattling breath and faced toward the younger man. 'Boy . . . ?'

'That there's the rock. Had to do it from behind when Sam was off his horse.'

The lawman felt for his tobacco, settled a cud in place, offered Damon the plug, and spat before speaking. 'Son of a bitch! Him'n me been friends a long time. Since I come to this gawddamned useless country. Empty his pockets, Damon.'

As the younger man knelt and went to work he looked up. 'Nothin', Walt. Even his clasp knife's gone.'

'Get on your horse, boy.'

'We can't just leave him here, Walt.'

'The hell we can't. All right, lend me a hand, we'll roll him into the brush.' As the large man leaned to roll he also said, 'This wasn't just some damned highbindin' grub-line rider. He wasn't alone. Push, boy. Harder!'

They got the corpse far enough into the snarled buckbrush, they also wasted more time looking for his horse until the marshal disgustedly said, 'Leave him be. Nothing's goin' to find him. Get on your horse. It'll be daylight before we reach his yard.'

The idea of abandoning the dead man did not sit lightly on Damon's conscience but he got back astride and for the remaining distance he scarcely spoke but his companion did.

Walt went to work exploring possi-bilities. He could understand what had happened back yonder but he could not satisfactorily explain to himself why it had happened.

Old Sam was harmless. As far as Damon could imagine he had no enemies, certainly none who would crush his skull, unless it was some saddle tramp who happened to be using the trail that ended in Sam's yard.

Damon, who had been watching for a lighted window up ahead, made an identification by scent. He never did see lamplight.

Kimball was older, tougher, less stunned by the appearance of death. He eventually detected the rough dawn-shadowed outline of an old log house with its customary assortment of a huge log barn and a scattering of lesser structures. The reason neither man had seen light was because they were approaching the yard from the rear.

A horse nickered in the onward distance. That soft trumpeting caused other horses to sound off.

Damon was piecing together what he

saw. His companion reacted differently. Kimball knew the Crawford yard, where the horse noise came from, and smiled mirthlessly. There were at least four horses in a corral, possibly more. Their racket would alert whoever had ridden those animals that someone might be coming. He jerked his head as he spoke, 'Angle more easterly, Damon. They heard them horses. Follow me.' Walt changed course and the horse-noise had no sequel.

They were sufficiently distant not to make noises that would rouse people as they progressed at a slow walk in the direction which would hide them from listeners up ahead.

The buildings were old, unkempt and warping in places where someone had piled stove wood.

Walt drew rein at the north-west corner of the big barn. Walt swung off, tossed his reins to Damon and told him to get down and to mind the horses. He showed the younger man how to use one hand to stifle any nickering their animals might make. His last words were given very quietly.

'I done some guessin' on the ride out here after we found Sam. That Texas cowman got the old man to head for home. He, or one of his men, cold-cocked him where we come onto him. The rest of it I figure they maybe already had in mind. Get Sam heading right, got rid of him, an' continued on to the yard to rummage. Old screwts like Sam with no banks close, hide their money. Maybe in the walls or in a hole ... that's what they're doin' now; ransackin' for Sam's cache. Now you mind these horses. I'll do a little scoutin' an' come back directly. Stay right here, boy, an' make no noise.'

The marshal was already moving when Damon stopped him. 'Two guns is better'n one, Walt.'

Kimball was disgusted but it didn't show. The night was not yet softening toward daylight, but when he started away again with no additional comment Damon understood.

The horses were hungry and did everything horses do to get the idea across. The longer Damon had to wait the more impatient he became. Damon became more troubled when a loud noise came from the house.

Having never owned a watch he had relied on the sun and moon; they were only haphazardly reliable and waiting had never proven to be satisfactory. This particular time Damon thought more time had passed than it had but a faint brightening of the sky helped. By his estimate dawn was coming.

He tethered the horses, crept inside the old log barn, found a large pan, filled it with rolled barley from a grain barrel and went back to slip bridles and divide the feed between the horses. It helped but half a panful encouraged the horses to want more. He dropped the empty large pan at the same moment he heard riders. The barn made it difficult to discern from which direction he heard ridden horses.

A dozen probabilities came to mind

but until he could place the horse-sounds he struggled to control his anxiety. A horse nickered. Damon edged to the furthest corner to wait for a repetition. The horse did not repeat itself. He turned to go back and nearly fell over something that had not been there earlier. Whatever it was came sluggishly upright. Damon swung hard. Whatever he had hit struck the barn's rear wall, rolled along it and fell.

Damon used one booted foot to kick with. Whatever he had connected with made a groan through clenched teeth. Damon leaned, got a fistful of cloth and heaved his opponent up against the logs. It was a man whose legs were buckling. Damon used both hands to push the man along the log wall until some of that watery pale light made the shadow assume a shape.

Damon could not prevent his half sigh, half groan. He held the man briefly in the wide barn-opening, then let go. The man crumpled like a wet blanket. Improving visibility made partial recognition possible. The man he had hit was the village's sometime freighter. His name was Hal White. What made it possible for a man as muscular as the freight hauler to have his stumbling unsteadiness, was the result of partially emptying the bottle of pop skull he had brought with him when he had joined the raiders.

Damon rummaged for something inside the barn to tie his captive with. He found a thirty-foot handmade horsehair lass rope. Damon dragged White where the horses were and tied him by the ankles with both arms in back.

The freighter swore and writhed. Damon cold-cocked him with the butt of his sidearm and hunkered with the limp man until he began to show evidence of recovering after which he yanked the man into a sitting position and slammed him hard with his back to the log wall. White caught his breath and stared. He had known the village roustabout for several years. He managed to gasp a name. 'Tuft! Damon — '

Damon slapped his face and snarled, 'How many you come out here with? Answer or I'll bust your head open!'

The freighter answered, 'Don't know exactly . . . '

'Are they in the house?'

'Set me to watch from the loft. I seen whoever's with you go skulkin' toward the corral. Finished the bottle and figured to drop on you, but missed. Damon? Is thcre somethin' hid out herc?'

Damon offered no answer as a burly half light, half shadow crossed inside the barn over hay or whispery straw and Damon fisted his handgun as he prepared to intercept whoever had entered the barn.

He did not cock the six-gun as he pressed into shadows and waited.

The man in the barn stopped just short of the rear barn opening, was still and silent a moment before making a husky growl.

'Damon? Show yourself, boy.'

Damon obeyed by inching around the rear opening. He ordinarily would have been unable to recognize the marshal. Daylight was coming but Walt was inside where no dawn-light reached.

Walt spoke again, in less of a whisper this time. 'Boy . . . ?'

Damon answered. 'I got Hal White out back. Trussed like a shoat. He's been drinkin'. Come along.'

Damon spoke those last two words while holstering his six-gun.

White had fought his bindings until he had fallen sideways. At sight of the marshal he pitched and heaved to sit up. He was not successful until the massive village lawman had leaned to help, then he said, 'Walt, for Chris'sake cut me loose. This halfwit clubbed me down'n tied me hard'n fast.'

Kimball straightened up, and struck.

White's head went violently sideways. He recovered and swore. Walt cocked his hand to strike again but this time

140

when he swung the trussed freighter anticipated the blow and reared so violently back and sideways the marshal's hand rattled over barn-siding logs. He didn't touch the freighter. Marshal Kimball cocked his fist to swing again. White spouted words one over the other.

'Len bossed it. He knew the old man had two caches without knowin' exactly where they was. I rode out a time or two an' drank with Sam. They figured I might know where he hid things. They didn't take me into the house, they left me to keep watch.'

The lawman had a fresh question. 'Hal, who killed Sam?'

This time the freighter squirmed before answering. 'It warn't me. I tell you on my honour. It warn't me!'

'Who, Hal? For the last time. Who!'

White sat totally still when he said, 'Len.'

'Len? How Hal?'

'Him'n another feller I didn't know, they rode up ahead talkin'. The other feller said he had to pee. We all stopped. Sam was fixin' to offer a bottle around . . . ' White fished for words. 'The feller who stopped to pee come up behind him holdin' a fair-sized boulder. When he brought it down old Sam went down with it. I squawked. They said Len could find the ol' man's hidin' places.'

Walt looked long at the man nearest to him, looked away without saying a word.

Damon had a question for the freighter. 'Hal, it don't make sense them not takin' you into the house with 'em.'

No one took up the valid argument of Damon because a gunshot sounded in the direction of the old house which by this time was being bathed from top to bottom in weak golden morning light.

Someone yelled. It was accompanied by the call of a name.

'Harry! Fur Chris'sake . . . '

The sobering freighter sat fixed in

place as though he was carved of stone. He whispered a name. 'Len!' The marshal sank to one knee gesturing with his hand in the prisoner's face. 'Hal! I counted six of 'em . . . '

The prisoner's stunned silence yielded to the hand in front of his face. 'It'd be maybe Len found the cache. An' someone shot him.'

Walt Kimball straightened up and scowled at Damon. 'We can leave this one. Did he have a Winchester?'

Damon shook his head as he went to work freeing up the captive's shellbelt. He did not believe leaving the blacksmith unguarded was a good idea but said nothing. If White could free himself it would have to be a miracle. Damon had thrown and tied enough bull calves for local ranchers to have mastered the art of using a pigging string. He started away. The marshal hesitated but only briefly. There was another gunshot at the house. The marshal forgot all about the trussed freight hauler.

Damon hesitated at the south-east corner of the barn where Walt was preparing to tell him to let Walt lead off; he had made a thorough scout of the old house during the time he had been separated from the horse-minding younger man.

Damon used the corralled horses as his shield as he went part way around the corral toward the house. As could be expected from the old house with its corrals and other typical outbuildings, the shelter was adequate; beyond the network of using-corrals and a small building beyond the corrals which was a well-house. Beyond that the distance to the main house was two yards.

The well-house was a regular four-sided and roofed-over house. In old Sam's case the well-house had been built twice as large as most ranch well-houses were.

There was a reason for that too. A well-house was always cool in both summer and winter.

Damon's problem was his feeling

that this particular well-house was easily twice the normal size, which meant he had to try sidling along the west side to reach the front, where the door was.

If anyone was watching from the house, a reasonable expectation now that daylight had returned, meant a stranger trying to get inside would be likely to get himself shot.

8

Searchers

Damon leaned to study the house. It was no longer dark but neither was there the shadowed outline of someone peering in the direction of the yard. To be certain he threw his hat which hit the northerly logs and fell to the porch. He waited. Next came his jacket, with the same results except that the coat being heavier it slashed across the siding with a solid sound.

Damon fisted his six-gun and waited. Nothing happened nor did anyone arrive at a window.

Walt slid to a halt and raised a restraining arm — too late.

Damon made a wild charge and did what his friend had expected to hear some-one else do, the solid sound of booted feet rattling the warped dry old porch floor.

He barely touched down before he threw himself sideways which rattled loose old porch planking.

He raised his sidearm and drew back the gun hammer, scarcely breathing. Someone inside the house made an audible exclamation. 'Over here! I told you there'd be someone follow us.'

Damon pressed close and flattened himself, six-gun rising. He neither saw nor heard anyone, cased up slightly, raised the pistol and could hear the reverberations beyond the old warped siding. He briefly held his breath. It was a short moment. A different voice spoke, slightly louder.

'It's the horses . . . listen!'

The standoff seemed to last an eternity. Damon shifted his gun hand, wiped the sweaty right hand and otherwise did not move. There should have been more than two of them. There was; a third man spoke with a higher, squeaky voice. 'How many you reckon?'

There was no answer until someone

either dropped or knocked a pan to the floor. That caused the first speaker to say, 'Who'd it be?'

Squeaky high voice answered. 'Rats! These old houses got rats. Where I grew up in Dodge City an' helped my pa patchin' up these old places we come on to rat burrows an' runs from the cellar to the top floor.'

The gruff intruder who had spoken first sounded less anxious than annoyed when he abruptly said, 'All right, Mello. You go back upstairs where we was searchin' an' go back to it.'

Squeaky voice sounded relieved when he said, 'Good idea. It's hot downstairs. I'm goin'.'

A soundless phantom pushed forth one foot close to the edge of the porch. Damon heard nothing until someone spoke in a whisper.

'You got 'em in the kitchen, Damon.'

The startled younger man was shifting his pistol before he knew who had spoken, but there was no mistaking that voice; it was the marshal.

'Follow me, boy. We can sidle around to the rear of the house.'

As the older man moved, Damon did also and heard Walt gasp and pull away. Damon followed as the larger man hissed, 'For Chris'sake be careful. I'm in my stockin' feet!'

Damon allowed his companion to get a lead of several feet. When it was possible to do so he looked down and sure enough the marshal would have been barefoot except for his socks.

Passing from the front to the back was not difficult. The house's west wall had no window. Damon was thankful for that. He was too young to understand why. When old Crawford had built his old house glass windows had been prohibitively expensive on the frontier.

The rear of the house had two windows, one smaller than the other one. The smaller window shed light into a storeroom. The larger one was on the east side of the powerfully built rear door.

Damon appreciated the marshal's caution when Walt stopped at a shielded small rear porch.

The marshal hesitated at the door, pressed close and after a moment, said, 'How many's supposed to be in there?'

Damon made a guess. 'Supposin' when them two shots was fired inside someone likely got hit. I'd say there're four or five . . . not countin' White maybe four . . . I don't know.'

Kimball said no more, but he raised splayed fingers to signal for Damon to stay where he was and without so much as a slither moved toward the furthest window. Damon watched. He wasn't really frightened.

Walt Kimball drew his Colt, hunkered lower at the window and froze. In the area of the corrals a horse made a snapping lunge at another horse. Whether he connected or not, a horse scattered gravel getting clear.

Walt straightened up slowly, winced at the pain in his back which was the result of being bent over so long, and shook his head. Damon gestured for them to continue on around to the far side and followed when Walt began moving, occasionally flinching; in gritty soil it made no difference whether a stalker was barefoot or wearing socks.

Damon hoped they would find no more windows. There wasn't but there was a door leading from an inside room to a small porch where a pair of rawhide slatted chairs were in place, close enough to a railing for a man to rest his feet.

While they were approaching those chairs the marshal paused to say, 'I think that room behind the door is where old Sam bedded down.'

That speculation heightened Damon's anxiety. No matter how many men were inside, it would be more than two. He closed up the distance between them, got too close for the marshal's appreciation, so Walt turned and snorted. Damon gave way.

There was a sound of booted feet coming down a stairwell. Damon pressed close and stopped. The sound eventually diminished. A man's voice replaced the former sound when he said, 'We got to burn this damned place. Harry, you do any good?'

Damon and Walt were able to put a name on one of the men inside . . . Harry Lincoln. He answered with the same voice the previous insider had used. 'Not until we're plumb sure. If it ain't down here nor up there that leaves them outbuildings. Maybe the barn or the well-house.'

'We already searched them, Harry. Maybe it's buried.'

This time the conversation ended in long silence. Whatever was the purpose for the room behind the door, the men inside it were soundless until someone called from up the stairs where there was a scuffed landing. 'Harry? There's a little low cupboard back up here.'

Now there was activity made not just by someone who wore spurs but by at least two men who did not wear them but sounded solidly hard as men crowded going back up the stairs.

Walt twisted until Damon could see his wide grin. He whispered, 'That's where old Sam kept fat wood for makin' fires when the snow was deep.'

As the marshal was resuming his earlier position against the outer wall Damon caught his sleeve and held it, his head cocked. The sound was unmistakable, loping horses coming from the direction of the village.

Walt's grin wiped itself out as he cocked his head. When he was satisfied he said, 'Who in hell?'

Damon did not speculate but being in sight on the east side of the house convinced him their visibility was not in their favour. He said, 'The barn!'

Kimball agreed without saying so. He was reluctant to abandon being this close to the men in the house but he stepped away and led a barefooted rush back the way they had come. When they were behind the house again the sound of loping horses was less discernible without dying altogether. The marshal didn't slacken until he reached the westerly corner, then he hesitated briefly long enough to be convinced the newcomers had not yet reached the yard, then led off again, with more prudence this time. He spoke huskily to the younger man following and said, 'By now everyone around figures what's goin' on, boy.'

'Walt, they come to help?'

The marshal gave one of his stifled snorts before saying, 'Help, like hell! Folks been guessin' for ten years that ol' Sam hid his money. Run, boy. Run hard!'

Damon ran. He passed the marshal at the storehouse which was where it had occurred to the marshal to shed his boots, and Walt did not catch up until they were again behind the big old barn, and then he grabbed Damon to stop him until they were plumb certain their trussed prisoner was still there.

The man they had left looped securely was not there but the hair rope was. It had been chewed through. Walt made a grimace and expectorated. Anyone who would chew all the way through a horsehair rope had to be desperate enough to do something like that.

The dust was churned where Damon leaned to locate boot prints. What he found was prints heading toward the corral. He would have followed but Walt stopped him. Of the corralled saddle-stock there was one animal making noise at the trough where it was drinking wearing a bridle.

Walt said, 'Gone, boy. He's had enough time to be dang near out of the country.'

Damon threw out an arm and swore under his breath. A saddle with both cinches flung over the cantle was lying in the dirt where other thirsty animals were softly snorting, heads down and still stiff-leggedly pawing. Damon left Kimball at the trough and started back but this time his direction was back toward the barn only until they veered to the right as they approached the

155

south-west corner of the barn and went around toward the front.

Damon back-tracked to follow the fresh sign. If it had still been dark he wouldn't have been able to. The tracks led alongside the barn to the front — and inside.

Damon gestured and Walt left the corral. Where they came together Damon stopped, raised his head and pointed upwards. Walt looked and scowled as he shook his head. Damon leaned and whispered, 'Took a while to bite through that rope. He was fixin' to rig that horse he'd already bridled, heard us an' run for it back here. You stay down here, Walt. I'm goin' up to the loft.'

The marshal whispered back, 'You're crazy. If he was up there when we come back why didn't he shoot?'

They were entering the barn when Damon answered, 'An' let the other ones know where we was?'

Walt started moving as he repeated something he had already said, 'Boy, you're crazy.'

Damon went as far as the loft ladder before he stopped. They both stood down there looking up. There was not a sound, not even the customary scuttling sound of foraging varmints, something everyone had heard in a barn with feed in the loft. Walt stopped scowling and whispering as Damon reached for the first rung.

Climbing a loft ladder with a six-gun in one hand was an awkward undertaking but anyone who had ever forked feed from a barn loft knew it could be done. Damon's confidence was supported by his conviction that Hal White, their former prisoner, had no weapon, which was to overlook that any freighter was bound to be properly muscled up, and cornering such an individual was the equivalent to cornering a she-bear with hungry cubs.

Damon had never heard the saying about burning bridges behind one, but after he had reached the top rung and was overwhelmed by the wonderful aroma of curing hay he leaned far over and gestured for Walt to remove the ladder.

Because the sun was climbing there were sprinklings of sunlight reaching through the shrinking logs. Damon remained flat until he could take advantage of the light.

He saw no one. Mounds of curing hay made for a difficult sighting in an area where the only sound came from near the northerly end of the sketchily lighted loft.

He remained on all fours until he was satisfied of the location of the only other person in the loft before he resumed his careful advance toward his adversary. The man he knew was unarmed not only surprised him but also shocked him. The gunshot being confined inside the sloping loft reverberated with the thunder of a cannon. Damon fired back, saw a wisp of dry wood explode upwards and sprang sideways. Before his adversary in the loft was ready for the next shot, Damon got himself up on all fours and launched himself toward the area he had seen gun-flash. It was close. One side of Damon's shirt tore loose and half turned him with the impact. He swung his right hand, felt the jolt when his pistol barrel connected with something that yielded inches. White cried out, sprang away with Damon desperately lunging to avoid the gunhand he could not see but knew had to be coming. Instead of cocking for another shot he used his Colt as a club. His opponent made a rough sound and collapsed.

For Damon it was over except for the wet, warm sensation on one side.

He groped, got a firm hold and swung the Colt again. This time there was no reaction, he had hit the man without being sure where. He got up as best he could, used both hands to get a firm grip and dragged his adversary where there was a fairly wide splinter of light.

Hal White, the freighter, was not only bleeding, but his breathing sounded like an injured bull, gasping unsteadily, and as though expelling breath was difficult and required some effort.

Damon dragged him in the direction of the loft hole, softly he called. 'It's Hal White.'

The man down below gave an answer totally lacking in surprise. He said, 'All right . . . are you hurt?'

'Winged on the left side. It don't hurt but it's bleedin'.'

'Come on down.'

'What about White?'

'Slide him down the ladder hole.'

'That could break his neck.'

'Good riddance.'

Damon wrestled the unconscious man around until his legs were protruding, burrowed under, used one arm to brace himself and gently groped for the second rung. The first rung gouged him in the stomach.

Walt's disgust was clear. 'You're goin' to fall with him. Let go, boy, let the son of a bitch fall.'

Damon could have complied but

held his breath while feeling for the next step.

The only difficulty he encountered was with the stocky man's shoulders. He was tempted to leave the freighter wedged there but twisted, turned, and got one shoulder through, then the other one and felt for the next step.

About the time he felt White slipping, the man below said, 'Jettison, boy, grip the sides with both hands an' let him fall.'

It was an unnecessary scrap of advice. White's weight overbalanced Damon partially to one side and Damon lowered that part of himself.

It was not far to fall. Damon heard air pump out of the freighter when he landed flat out on his back.

Marshal Kimball swore, hesitated just long enough to make sure Damon would not also fall, then stepped past, straddled White with his Colt pointing downward. White did not move until Damon was on the ground brushing himself off.

Walt said, 'He had a gun?'

'I never saw it.'

'You're bleedin' like a stuck hawg. Come over to the light.'

The wound was one of those injuries that bled like rain without being dangerous. Walt tore a sleeve off the freighter, tied it around Damon, and watched until the bleeding diminished, then said, 'Go watch the front, Damon.'

Those riders who had been riding toward the yard had also heard gunshots in the loft. They had the barn surrounded and cut off from old Sam's house.

One of them sang out soon as Damon appeared inside the barn near the doorway. He called out, 'Who'n hell are you? What you doin' in the barn?'

Walt left off tying Hal White who was beginning to recover from being senseless. As White felt his binding and saw the six-gun twelve inches from his chest, he stopped fighting the rope, looked straight up and said, 'Kimball?'

Walt didn't answer, he leathered his

weapon, leaned to make sure White couldn't get free, stood over him to briefly push his finger in the downed man's body as he softly said, 'Not a gawddamned word out of you. Understand? Don't even groan.'

The marshal joined Damon back a short distance from the wide barn opening and said, 'Is that you, Dudley?'

The reply was slow coming. 'Yeah.'

'Get out where I can see you.'

'Walt? I can make out both of you. What in hell is goin' on out here?'

'Dud, how many fellers are with you?'

'Walt, you answer questions, I'll ask 'em. How'd you come to be out here? I got some boys from the village'n my three riders. Seven of us, Walt. Who's in the house?'

'Ol' Sam's dead.'

'We know that. Some kids out huntin' squirrels found him. Walt . . . ?'

'Dud, I'm not plumb sure what it's all about, but those fellers in the house — '

'Who are them fellas, Walt? Cattle buyers from out of the country?'

'Dud, listen to me. I got Damon in here with me. I got a prisoner. If you want to chance it, come an' see for yourself.'

This time a reply was delayed longer. 'You come out if you want to, but we're not comin' in there. There's a couple of fellers roustin' around outside . . . lookin' for you maybe. You just set tight. We'll poke aroun' an' talk to you later. Walt? Don't shoot until one of us talks to you again. Understand?'

Walt and Damon exchanged a look before Damon said, 'All right. We'd maybe get to shootin' at each other. Suits me, Walt.'

The marshal called that he and his companion in the barn would shoot only if they had to. He finished giving that assurance by also saying, 'Be real careful, Dud. We figure those ransackin' bastards in the house are huntin' for old Sam's cache . . . if he had one.'

The marshal led off back to the place

where the freighter seemed not to have moved. He knelt to untie White's hands and arms then got Damon to lend a hand as they dragged White where he would have a support for his back.

White had heard the conversation up near the front of the barn and while brushing himself off and gingerly exploring his injuries he said, 'Walt? Is that the same Dudley feller who owns the Circle D outfit east of town?'

Damon answered while Walt was coiling the tie rope.

'It's him, Hal. I've hayed for him over the years. I'd know his voice in hell. His full name is Cole Dudley.'

White was massaging his arms when next he spoke. 'Did you know that son of a bitch used to ride with the Younger boys?'

Walt snorted while pushing himself back upright. 'Hal, I've heard that story at least fifty times. Dud never rode with outlaws. I back-tracked him not long after he bought into this country. Hal, who is that *Tejano* cattle buyer?'

'Damned if I know but the feller got me in this mess is named Baxter. He plans for 'em. Got three or four bands rustled for him an' he peddles the stock they bring him over the line into Canada. You liked to cut off all my circulation with that damned tie rope. Walt, did Len hire out to rustle Sam Crawford's cattle? After all the time Len's rode for old Sam I can't be sure why he'd sell out like that. Sam was old. Old Sam liked Len an' paid well. An' I believe Len liked Sam.'

Walt looked at Damon and shook his head without speaking. What the captive had said was worth considering.

Hal White stopped rubbing his arms and suggested going as far as the corral, rig out a horse and get the hell out of the country.

When Damon and the marshal were alone, Damon said, 'What'll happen to old Sam's outfit includin' his special cattle?'

The marshal had no comment. He and the old man had been close over

166

the years. It bothered him to think about Sam Crawford being dead. He and Sam had sat in Sam's filthy kitchen many a cold winter night seeing which one could out-cheat the other at cards.

They'd talked those nights away on many subjects including old Sam's lack of heirs.

The day was wearing along. Those ransackers over at the house had used Dudley's intrusion to good purpose but despite tearing into furniture and walls they had not found a cache.

9

Cougars Howl at Night

The arrival of more men brought a silence in the house and throughout the yard. Walt told Dudley what they had been doing since their earlier arrival. The rancher, a medium-sized man, ran cattle east of the village. Like other inhabitants of the area he only visited the hamlet for mail and the supplies he did not have to go further to find.

He was a married man with a wife as well as a brace of half-grown boys. His sons and a pair of men rode for him. They were with him today; they listened to the town marshal as solemn as owls, until one son made a suggestion that Walt Kimball scowled about. He said, 'Pa, countin' us'uns we can charge over there ashootin' an' smoke 'em out, if there ain't no more'n the marshal says.'

Walt spoke before the elder Dudley got a chance.

'Boy, if there's only a couple of 'em, that's twelve bullets. A blind man firin' off twelve rounds would hit one of us, an' maybe all of us.'

The rawboned youth gave a sulky retort. 'Me'n Asa could sneak around back an' — '

Walt interrupted, 'Boy, they're maybe not all in the house. We stirred 'em up before we got back here.'

The rawboned youth replied, 'Are you sayin' we rode into the yard with them bastards where they could see us?'

'Somethin' like that,' the lawman replied; he faced the eldest newcomer and gently wagged his head. Youth had its advantages but under the present circumstances what was needed was caution not rashness.

While they were palavering in the barn there was a drum thunder of hooves and the youth named Asa sprang to the wide front barn opening. A pair of horsemen were leaving the yard in a belly-down run. Cole Dudley got beside his son and used a strong-armed gesture to stop Asa from raising the six-gun he had drawn.

Damon reached the doorway as Asa's father said, 'No, you idiot! You miss an' you're goin' to hit his horse.'

The rawboned youth faced his father as angry as a hornet. 'I wouldn't have missed,' he snarled.

The men on foot watched the pair of horsemen throw up curls of dun dust, almost enough to hide the riders.

As Damon whirled he threw out an arm to brush Walt Kimball. Without a word Damon ran out the back of the barn and stood in the direction of the corral where loose stock was lined up side by side watching the escaping men become half size with the sun making identification impossible.

Walt was rigging out his horse when Damon yelled at him. 'Duck! That son of a bitch's got a carbine.'

The man Damon called about was on the front porch like he seemed to have taken root. When Damon yelled he was raising his Winchester.

They were not the only men who saw the escapees; the man with the carbine was snugging it to his shoulder when a flurry of gunshots broke the hush and the man on the porch hadn't quite snugged back his saddle gun when the bullets hit him. He dropped his carbine, faced toward the front of the barn where the Dudleys had fired, began facing back when both his legs buckled under him.

The escaping men were lost to sight. Damon looped the reins inside the corral, vaulted out of the corral and reached the downed man on the veranda before he expired and used his bent leg as a prop. The man looking up at Damon tried to smile. He only succeeded part way before his eyes paled to a dull milkiness and his breath ran out.

Two men in the corral finished what Damon and Walt had been doing before one man yelled to open the corral gate.

Walt was bending over the limp man Damon was holding up and swore. The Dudley boys went out of the yard nearly side by side. Their father yelled at them as they flashed past; they either did not hear him or possibly heard him and ignored the yell.

As the yard returned to its earlier stillness, Dudley walked over from the barn looking to his left until he reached the first step, then hesitated as he recognized the dead man. He said, 'That's Len, for Chris'sake. What was he doin' inside the house?'

Walt whose back was to the others while he squinted in the direction those riders had gone, spoke without turning around. 'Len . . . ? He somehow got inside?' He faced around. 'They would've killed him. He should have waited until we stormed the house. He more'n likely couldn't have taken them by himself.'

Damon stood up looking at Walt, who returned the look without blinking.

The only way old Sam's range boss

could have been inside the house without being detected was if he was one of the raiders.

Dudley broke the hush. 'We'll give him a right proper send off. I knew Len since I come into the country. He'd been old Sam's eyes an' ears more years than I like to look back on.'

Walt and Damon left the Dudleys at the house, caught their own animals and rode in pursuit of the raiders at an easy, mile-eating lope.

Not until they had passed the thicket where old Sam had been concealed did either of them speak. Then Damon said, 'Somethin' wrong about Len being inside with them others.'

Walt covered a fair distance before he replied. 'Boy, Len had been with the old man at least ten, twelve years, maybe more, as a hired hand. When a man works that long for someone . . . '

Damon mulled over that before looking over at Walt.

Walt glanced over at Damon and said, 'Damon, I don't for a minute believe Len was in cahoots with them rustlers.'

'But . . . ?'

Walt continued as if Damon hadn't interrupted. 'I believe they somehow got the drop on Len and took him with them to force him into tellin' where old Sam had hid his cache, but it didn't work. Did you see the bruises on his face? I think they worked him over good inside the house. I also think Lincoln wasn't what he said he was. I think he had more men in on this and hadn't planned on payin' for Sam's cattle.'

Damon sighed. That made more sense to him and seemed to bring a feeling of relief. Maybe everyone didn't like Len but most did, including Damon.

They had village rooftops in sight before Damon spoke again. He said, 'Mister Dudley, how you reckon he knew?'

Walt dropped back to a steady walk. Damon's horse took his cue and also slackened. Walt did not look at his companion when he said, 'Looks to me like someone turned them cattle loose.'

Damon stood in his stirrup and sure enough the gate was open and the corralled cattle were gone. Not just gone, but were nowhere in sight. Damon eased down, 'Who'd you reckon did that?'

Walt wagged his head without commenting but he had something else in mind and twisted in the saddle when he spoke. 'Boy, I been tryin' to keep track. Them two Mexicans that rode with the Texan make three. Dud an' his crew makes another five. There was them others that come out first, probably more of Lincoln's men. Seems to me couple of them got shot. Damon, two stole the horses Dud and his lads run off on . . . how many you expect was alive when we left?'

'Dud's boys an' them two as got away while we was talkin' in the barn . . . that's maybe six.'

They were wrangling over the

number of survivors when Damon abruptly set his horse up and said, 'Son of a bitch!'

He did not explain what had startled him. Walt Kimball saw the three riders coming toward them from the village. They were dusty, faded-looking strangers. The only distinctive thing about the trio was the badge on the shirt front of one of them, the man with a trimmed russet beard and long hair showing in the back of his head. This man raised a gloved hand. Walt growled, the one thing he did not appreciate at the moment was a delay to palaver with strangers. But he drew rein, halted and rested both hands on the saddle horn.

The bearded man with the un-shiny badge was reining down as he offered a greeting.

'Good mornin', gents. I'm Sheriff Jeff Cutler from up Montana way. In that town back yonder a couple of gents told me their town lawman was out here a piece, most likely at a ranch belongin' to a feller named Samuel Crawford.

We're lookin' for a couple of men who might be in the area.'

Neither lawman offered a hand to be shaken. Walt Kimball was expressionless while he delayed comment. He eased a foot out of his stirrup, and considered the other two strangers.

Walt Kimball was dog-assed tired. At his best he was not a quick thinker. This moment his answer was delayed for as long as was required to get a sliver of tobacco accommodated before he said, 'I'm town marshal hereabouts. Name's Walt Kimball. These fellers you lookin' for . . . they got names?'

The Montanan replied curtly. He was the opposite of Walt, he was not only a quick thinker but delays irritated the hell out of him. His reply was brisk. 'I got no idea what names they might be goin' by down here, but where we come from they called themselves James Tohey and Gordon Sheffler.'

Walt shook his head and raised his reins. 'Never heard of 'em, Sheriff, but the ground's dry enough for trackin'. Good luck.'

The Montanans did not yield so Walt and Damon had to ride out and around them.

Once, Damon looked back. The Montanans were in a loose lope heading for the Crawford place.

When they reached the village, the sun was beginning to slant away toward afternoon. Walt left Damon at his office, was gone long enough for that ponderously weighty sun to slant away in the west.

Damon was hungry. He quenched his thirst with a long drink from the marshal's hanging *olla* and was rehanging it from its hook when Walt walked in. He went to the littered old table that served as a desk, sat down, eyed the younger man stoically and leaned across holding out an envelope.

Damon took the paper, sat down to open it and said, 'I'm hungry,' and sat there like a carving. He turned the paper over and turned it back. Walt sat like a Buddha, unmoving, savouring his tobacco and watching the younger man. Eventually Damon looked up. He had high colour in his face.

Walt cleared his throat, took out his six-gun, dug in a battered cigar box for the implements and went to work cleaning the gun when Damon said, 'Gawd a'mighty . . . Walt?'

Damon arose with the paper in one hand. Walt said, 'Sit down, boy, it's not every day a feller goes from sometimes sleepin' in hay lofts an' eatin' leftovers. *Boy, sit down!*'

Damon sat, raised the paper to reread it and said, 'Somebody's joshin' me?'

Walt shook his head. 'After you get fed, we'll go back an' if anyone's pokin' around we'll run 'em off.'

Damon held the paper in his lap staring straight at the marshal. 'I . . . don't believe this.'

Walt did not raise his eyes from what he was doing when he said, 'Believe it, Damon. Sam give me that paper

. . . must be nigh on to two, three years back. In fact I helped him write it.'

'Why me, Walt?'

'Well, boy, it was his to do with as he wanted to an' him havin' no family, he got pretty fond of you. He once told me of all the fellers he'd hired at the ranch you was the only one who kept smilin' when you was tired an' kept right on workin'.'

Damon read the paper again and spoke while doing so. 'We was friends. He asked me once to come live at the ranch.'

Walt dried gun oil off his hands using the same rag he'd cleaned the gun with, otherwise the only change was that his features relaxed. He almost looked pleasant. 'You own it, Damon. Lock, stock an' barrel. I got to say I wasn't convinced he'd out-live me. I told him that one time an' he said I'd inherit next if I'd find me a good widow woman with at least one workin'-size son.' Walt stood up, leathered his pistol, hitched both belts, the gunbelt and the belt holding up his britches and said, 'Damon, you set here until I round up some fellers to ride out there, but I expect we'd do better to wait for mornin' an' go alone.'

When Walt got to the door he stood in the opening and said, 'Boy, get used to it. I'll be back directly . . . Damon? You own it all, old Sam's land'n cattle includin' that band of belted critters . . . of which I think that's the craziest notion I ever heard of.'

Damon stood up, folded the paper, pocketed it and spoke. 'I'll get something to eat and go bed down. What about them sons of bitches that got away?'

'In the mornin'. Boy, you'd ought to sleep real good. My guess is that damned few men get up in the mornin' ownin' just about nothin' an' bed down ownin' more than danged few fellers get even if they work all their lives to get it . . . like old Sam did.'

For Walt Kimball this was about as long-winded a sermon as he had ever delivered. The oddest part of it was that when Damon bedded down in a barn loft he could have repeated it word for word.

Damon found a place to bed down, as good a place as he'd ever found so he should have slept, but in fact because he had a meal first and late, he could not sleep. Come predawn he was wide awake.

There were troughs where a man could make himself presentable. As he was finishing at the trough, an elderly widow woman hailed him with an offer of breakfast. He followed her into as neat and clean a kitchen as he'd ever seen, and ate. She talked like a bird hardly drawing breath until he interrupted, handed her the briefly worded letter granting him ownership in full for everything old Sam had owned.

It did not occur to him that everyone his hostess came in contact with before evening would know of his inheritance.

When he and the marshal were ready

to leave the village, Walt dropped another clanger. They took a short cut in the direction of the ranch and encountered old Sam's seasoned riders who had returned to their home place and were now concerned with finding old Sam.

Walt sat his horse like a rock until they had explained about their search at the bullet-holed old house, where they'd found a couple of dead men and now wanted their wages so they could leave the country. Damon got a surprise. Walt fished out a wad of greenbacks held together by a short length of oiled rawhide and with Damon and the cowboys watching, peeled off the money owed, handed it to the riders and with a curt nod to them raised his reins and continued to ride into the yard.

When they tied up at the house, Walt spoke in a toneless voice. 'Boy, as old Sam's heir you owe me the wages I paid them lads.' Walt grinned. 'Unless you'd care to hire me on, in which case you can just add it to my first month's wages.'

Damon laughed.

They did not expect to find live troublemakers out there and found none. The house had been ransacked until it looked like hostile tomahawks had been there. When Damon stood in the wrecked parlour Walt shook his head in disgust and said, 'If it's all the same to you, Damon, I'd as soon as not waste another day lookin' for what's not here, an' go where it is.'

Damon's mouth hung open. Walt leaned in the doorway connecting the parlour and the kitchen eyeing his companion. In after years, Damon would think that the older man had been enjoying himself. As they faced each other in the ruined old house, Damon had a fleeting feeling that Walt was being motivated by some inner sensation of difficult satisfaction, and he was right. He asked, 'You know something, Walt?'

Kimball's normal taciturnity came

close to cracking. 'When we was up at old Sam's line shack, I wanted to talk some sense to him . . . let's ride, boy.'

'Where? That Texan'll be so far off by now we couldn't catch him if we had wings, an' that other son of a bitch, that organized rustler-boss from 'way up north . . . '

Walt straightened up off the door jamb and reached inside his shirt to scratch as he looked steadily at Damon and spoke. 'To hell with that Texan. I didn't like his looks from the start. We'll have time to worry about him after we make another long ride.'

Damon's expression of bafflement showed but he followed the marshal outside where heat was coming into the day.

Walt said nothing as he took a shovel and a crowbar from the barn, handed the shovel to Damon, took the crowbar with him as he mounted his horse and reined westerly.

Damon said nothing. It was clear that the older man was not in a talkative mood, which was not entirely unusual.

They stopped at a creek to drink and water the horses only once after which Damon followed when Walt changed course, this time following the sign of horses and cattle northward.

The sun was slanting away when they had the old shack in sight, along with some cattle, several of which were belted and marked with old Sam's brand.

At the clearing, Walt off-saddled, turned his horse into the same corral he'd taken it out of a few days before, and jerked his head for Damon to do the same.

Inside, the cabin had a rank aroma. Damon left the door open as Walt dropped his hat on the table, sat down and finally spoke.

'Boy, while a man's gettin' older, some of his earlier notions just up'n leave him.'

Damon, whose disposition was normally easy-going to the point of indifference, sat opposite the marshal, fixed him with an unyielding stare and spoke for the first time in hours. 'Walt,' he said, 'I'm right fond of you, but lately you've been actin' downright strange. What in hell did you get me to pack that damned shovel up here for?'

Walt was fired up and showed it when he said, 'There's somethin' you never been taught, boy. Don't interrupt when someone is talkin'.'

Damon's face reddened, he clenched both fists. Walt noticed and leaned back off the old table and spoke in a soft tone. 'You been around quite a while. Old Sam took a likin' to you. There's things you don't know an' I expect Sam wouldn't like me tellin' you.' Walt paused. 'Sam was married young. His wife got him a little boy. That was in Missouri. Red Legs raided his staked-out land in Missouri. Sam was off cuttin' lodge poles to make another room on his soddie. He come home after dark, put up his team . . . there was no light in his soddie.

'He went to the house . . . his

187

woman'd been used up pretty bad an' run through with a big knife. The little boy must've hollered. He was choked to death.'

Damon's clenched fists tightened. 'Indians?'

'I told you: Red Legs. Fellers who maybe rode with Quantrill. Whiteskins . . . He spent a year huntin' 'em, an' never found 'em. Damon, from the first time he saw you he told me you was the spittin' image of his boy. Older, but a sure-shot look-alike. You want to know why he wanted to take you in? He was out of his head for a long time. He come to this country and tried to work himself to death.'

Walt stood up, picked up his hat and jutted his jaw in the direction of one of the wall bunks as he fished one of those little flat sardine tins from a pocket and tossed it on the table. 'That there is supper, Damon. Bed down on whichever of those bunks you want. In the mornin' we'll finish up here. Now, you eat, an' rest if you want to. I'm goin' outside . . . I figure to be alone for a spell.'

Damon did not move after the older man had closed the cabin door after himself, not until he heard Walt forking feed to the horses, then he took the piece of paper from a pocket, lighted what remained of a candle and hunched forward to read.

It was an awful lot for him — maybe for anyone — to make sense out of all he'd seen and done lately.

When Walt returned after dark, Damon was still at the table, hunched over with his face on the paper, sound asleep.

Walt kicked out of his boots, making no effort to be quiet about it, and spread out on the wall bunk nearest the stove. Some varmint, probably attracted by horse scent, prowled nearby and as it was leaving it sat back and sang to the moon. When Walt had been younger than Damon, folks had told him mountain lions slept at night, they only hunted and howled after daylight came.

He smiled, watched the candle stump burn itself down to a nubbin and flicker out.

In the morning he would do what he'd brought the boy up here to do and that would end his obligation to an old man who had been like kin to him.

10

Caught!

The scraps left over from their previous visit were scarcely edible and what remained of the two sardine cans of the night before did not constitute a suitable breakfast. Damon's offer of conversation in the morning was not successful. Walt grunted answers or gave none at all.

While they were saddling, Walt brought the tools from the shack, kept the crowbar for himself, handed the shovel to Damon, and led off heading eastward where Damon was pretty well occupied dodging tree limbs.

Walt's leadership left Damon about equal parts dodging and trying to figure out where they were going.

With the sun shadowing every

switchback and ravine, Damon eventually allowed his horse to follow in a head-down indifferent fashion.

They crossed a clearing where logs made litter. Someone had cut jackpines here many years earlier. The watercourse picked a way among the deadfall where old tracks remained. Damon found a cast horseshoe when his horse stirred water. He dismounted, retrieved the shoe and carried it along with him.

Later, Walt stopped at a spongy place where he used the shovel to dig a couple of feet down and when it filled with water they removed bridles and let the horses tank up. Walt drank there but Damon didn't. He hadn't roughed it enough in his life yet to have developed the art of drinking sump water using his teeth as filters.

They broke clear with the sun behind them and halted atop one of those old peaks where Indians had made arrowheads and left the chipped-off rocks.

Ahead, still easterly and below, was one of those burned-off places and two fair-sized log buildings. One was obviously a house, the other building was a barn.

The sound of chickens was barely discernible. Damon said, 'I'll be damned.'

Walt spat aside, grinned and spoke. 'Homesteaders, boy. I'd guess where they set down roots is where folks want to be far off from neighbours.' Walt settled both hands atop his saddle horn gazing thoughtfully down yonder.

Damon, with no idea where they were and hungrier than a bitch wolf wondered aloud if it would throw them off-trail if they went down there to ask about a meal. Walt shook his head, reined around and started back the way they had come. Damon said nothing for an hour or so, then he braced the older man. 'Walt, just what in hell are we doing?'

'Ridin', boy. I expect we didn't really have to come this far but better to be alive than dead.'

'Live or dead? What in hell are you talkin' about?'

Walt went along on loose reins for a spell before answering. 'Just in case we was followed.' Walt's reins were flapping. 'I wish I'd thought to bring more of them little fish along.'

Damon reddened and reined to a stop. 'I'm goin' to go southward . . . straight southward. I know there's places a man can get fed down there!'

The older man sat perfectly still eyeing the younger man. 'Boy, I come too far.' He wigwagged the reins and as his horse started moving he said, 'It's only a coupla miles back . . . tag along, Damon, an' you'll never regret it.'

Damon let Walt get a couple of yards ahead then eased up on his reins and kneed his animal to follow. His decision was simple. Having followed this far, if he did as he had threatened, split off and go southward, he would eventually find food, and he just might never know what he had missed.

They rode one behind the other for

a considerable distance before Walt abruptly yanked to a halt, dismounted, walked back to Damon and spoke very quietly. 'Get down an' don't rattle that shovel.'

Walt's expression was dead serious. When Damon was on the ground, Walt pointed to low limbs and led his horse to be tied. Damon was tethering his animal when Walt tapped his shoulder.

'That smoke's at the clearing. Most likely at the cabin.'

Damon watched the rising tuft of white smoke. 'How far?'

'Half a mile.'

Damon softly said, 'You was right.'

The older man lowered his gaze. 'That don't matter.'

'Who would it be?'

Walt hung fire before answering. 'Your guess is as good as mine, but we got to find out. I'd say they haven't been up here long. Bring the shovel an' don't make no noise.'

It made Damon uncomfortable leaving their horses but Walt was moving northward, his obvious intention to get north of the clearing, which made sense. Northward they would be able to have forest cover, the trees in that direction came down closest to the cabin.

They walked noiselessly, as far as possible before Walt raised an arm. A compact-looking horse met them without moving. He was as surprised as they were. Damon stood perfectly still hoping as hard as he could that the horse would not make a noise.

Walt was ahead, it was he who had come through forest gloom and now slowly turned toward Damon, and he did little more than whisper when he said, 'Can you see the left shoulder?'

Damon had to take several steps to see as much of the horse as Walt had seen. He saw what Walt looked at but couldn't read it. He said, 'Mex brand, Walt,' and got no clear configuration as the muscled-up horse turned to walk closer to its companion, a second horse, this one facing the wrong direction to show a marking, if there was one.

Walt walked northward until he was among large dun-coloured boulders. He had trees between himself and the shack. He leaned on a very large rock, waited until Damon was close then said, 'We got no Mex-branded horses in this country.'

Damon could have agreed, instead he said, 'There's likely three of 'em that belong to what's-his-name, that Texas cow buyer.'

Walt barely nodded his head. He had surmised the same thing. What he wondered about was how the Texan had managed to be up here, unless they had trailed Walt and Damon and that didn't make sense. The last time he'd seen the Texan and his *vaqueros* they were hightailing it in a different direction.

But the horse with the Mex brand hadn't come up here by himself. He had sweat marks.

Walt persisted in running things. He said, 'Stay here,' to Damon, and was moving clear when Damon stopped him. 'Hold it. *You* stay here. I'll scout around.'

Walt's brows dropped a notch. 'Boy, I've done this before an' — '

'Walt! I expect we should get it settled who is the head Indian . . . that's me, not you.'

Walt did not move while eyeing the younger man. Damon leaned the shovel aside and walked westerly. He did not feel good about establishing who was in charge but that mood lasted only until he saw a husky-built, swarthy shadow move along the back of the old line shack.

He very slowly dropped low and moved on an intercepting course. The stocky man's spurs occasionally rattled when they contacted rocks.

Damon stopped moving. At the rate the dark man was moving Damon would not be able to meet him.

He got closer by utilizing trees and thick shadows, drew his six-gun and straightened up south-east of the stocky man wearing the Mex spurs.

Because he made no noise it had to be movement that caught the other man's attention. Whatever it was the stocky man stopped walking and crouched. His right hand was dropping toward a holster when Damon said, 'Don't! Take your hand away from the pistol! Don't move!'

The man's right hand froze. He did not come out of his crouch as he turned his head slightly.

Damon spoke again. 'Walk toward me.' The man made no move to obey Damon's order. He seemed frozen in place.

Damon had never thrown down on anyone in his life. He was functioning by instinct. 'Drop the gun! *Drop it!*'

The man obeyed but very slowly. His sidearm made a rustling sound as it landed in bone-dry pine needles. He straightened up and spoke. 'Who are you? Which one . . . ?'

It was the accent and the way words were clipped off that let Damon know he had one of those Mexicans who had come north with the Texas cattle buyer. There had been two. One used English, the other one hadn't during their previous meeting. This *vaquero* was younger than the other one. Damon asked his name. The Mexican dawdled over answering. He clearly had not mastered English. Someday Damon would know how it was with people who used English only after they had repeated it to themselves in their own language before repeating it in English.

'My name is Estevan, *señor*. What is your name?'

Damon did not reply. He picked up the discarded six-gun, used it to steer his prisoner in the direction of Walt's huge boulders.

Walt looked from one of them to the other before asking Damon how he'd caught the *vaquero* and after Damon explained, Walt addressed Damon. 'What in hell are we goin' to do with him?'

Damon had thought about that as he'd been herding the man. 'Find out why he's up here, who he come with.'

The conversation was distinctly blighted but the Mexican did as well as he could in English. Walt and Damon caught one name that was repeated: Harry. Walt put a long look on the Mexican. 'Harry Lincoln.'

Damon's reply was curt. 'We knew that. Lincoln was the only one who brought Mexicans with him.' He did not wait for a reply, he said, 'How did you follow us?'

Before the prisoner could reply, Walt held up a hand for silence. Damon strained to hear and detected no sound, human or animal, until the cabin door was opened and closed. Walt pushed the Mexican away and moved in front of Damon with his six-gun cocked and raised.

Damon heard boot steps in gravelly soil. He began to face around. From the corner of his eye he saw Estevan crouch to run. Damon swung and Estevan struck the big boulder and slid down it to end up in a limp ball.

Whoever had left the cabin stopped stone still, raised his right hand with a pistol in it and froze.

There'd been no time to comment on the hearing ability of that man who had come out the cabin door but he had clearly heard Estevan's grating descent on the rock.

Walt whispered something unintelligible and called, 'Lincoln?'

The gun flash was audible but the call did not seem to have been heard.

Estevan jerked against the large rock he was slumped against.

Damon felt the passage of a bullet very close to the side of his head.

Walt fired back. A splinter tore out of the door and the man who had fired over there made some kind of squeal, dropped and rolled. Where he fetched up bellydown he raised up just enough to return the gunshot and this time Walt kicked away from a rotten stump that was shattered with wood punk flying in several directions.

Damon returned the shot and

ducked down and around a huge tan boulder. An abrupt flash of light from inside the cabin exposed the table and a lighted candle atop it. The door sagged badly from a broken hinge.

Walt yelled again. 'Leave your gun on the ground an' stand up!' The return gunshot had to be a sound shot and although Damon had never before been in a situation like this, he swore at his companion.

'Walt, for Chris'sake you're goin' to get us both killed.'

That was enough of a long-winded shout to provide someone with grounds for an excellent sound-shot. But no gunfire was returned. It was a snarling growl of an answer. 'Leonard? Is that you, range boss? Put up your damned gun. There's enough for both of us.'

Damon got closer to the marshal. 'Do like he says, Walt. I'll cover you.'

Walt leaned to whisper. 'Shut up! You'll get us both killed!'

Walt braced his right hand with the left hand and fired.

This time the man on the ground near the shattered door fired twice as rapidly as he could pull back the hammer and squeeze the trigger.

Damon rolled frantically, bumped into a flourishing fir tree with undergrowth fully around it.

He could make out the silhouette of the man near the cabin. Damon didn't fire. He sank to one knee and called. 'Lincoln! Look behind you where the door's hangin' open.'

The shot toward Damon's tree was the answer he got and almost simultaneously a single shot struck Damon's tree making green bark fly. Damon got lower and repeated what he'd said and this time it made a pair of shoulders and a head rise inches off the ground as the prone man got high enough to turn. It required no more than a few seconds for the gunman to see where the candlelight limned inside the line shack where a hatless Mexican was sprawled across the table.

Damon waited until the head and

shoulders got flat down then called to him by name. 'Mr Lincoln, you're alone. That one on the table's dead; the other one's knocked out of it against a big boulder.' Then Damon lied with a clear conscience. 'The others beside me — six of us — are goin' to blow your gawddamned head off unless you throw your gun as far as you can pitch it!'

Where Walt was flat out there was the echo of a groan. Walt hadn't been wounded, he was disgusted at that lengthy ultimatum. He added to it. 'Lincoln! You got five seconds.'

The answer was brusque. 'Six my butt! We tracked two of you!'

Walt called to Damon. 'Blow the bastard's head off, boy!'

Damon was concentrating on the flat-out man with the candlelight coming out that ruined door backgrounding his target. He took a steady rest on the rough bark of his fir tree. 'Last chance, mister!'

The backgrounded man said, 'Here it

comes!' and hurled his six-gun in Walt's direction.

It barely struck the ground before Walt said, 'Stand up! Hands over your head!'

The shadowy outline Damon had in his sights came slowly up off the ground, both arms raised.

Walt called to Damon. 'Go search the son of a bitch, boy!'

Most men would have waited a bit. Not Damon, he got upright, six-gun dangling and walked to where their second prisoner was soundless, standing. When they recognized each other the Texan snarled. 'If I'd known it was you I'd've run you down'n cracked your head!'

Damon went over his second captive, fished and held a wicked-bladed knife he'd taken from the man's right boot. Then he smiled, gave his captive a rough push toward Walt and said, 'How'd you come to follow us?'

For the second time Walt interrupted what might have been an answer. He said, 'Why'd you shoot the Mexican in the shack?'

The Texan lowered his arms as he answered. 'I didn't shoot him. Whichever you fellers shot through the door must have hit him.' The Texan's gaze was distracted when Estevan used the face of the boulder behind him to paw his way up to his feet. He said, 'Estevan . . .'

The *vaquero* faced around. He swore at Lincoln then used broken English. 'It goin' to be easy,' he said with anger in every word. 'We come with you up here an' drive back some especial cattle!'

Damon went toward Estevan and told him to be quiet. Estevan considered the man who had knocked him senseless, and sank back down on the ground in silence, the fight gone out of him.

Walt faced Lincoln. 'Why'd you follow us?'

The Texan had been thinking. Whatever happened henceforth would not be as he had thought it should. He put a narrowed look on the marshal. He said, 'From what I've heard there's plenty for all of us.'

Walt scowled. 'What've you heard an' who said it?'

'An old freighter told me there's talk Sam Crawford'n you made that tomb and planted that old buck atop it along with a bloody fortune under it.'

Walt looked scornful, but before he could speak the Texan beat him to it. 'When you'n the lad rode out of Crawford's yard — '

'You followed us,' Walt exclaimed and looked at Damon. 'We'll take 'em along. They can do the diggin', I'm dog-ass tired.'

Whatever the Texan and his *vaquero* thought they said nothing as they were gone over again for hideout weapons before being herded out to the burial place.

Lincoln leaned on the crowbar looking at Walt. 'All right, where do we dig?' He paused before also saying, 'How much is buried here?'

Walt ignored the question. He told Damon to watch the prisoners and began a slow, at times hesitant, shuffling walk around the old burial site. He didn't have to feel anxious about the captives, they and Damon watched every step he took.

He made that trip twice completely around the mound, sometimes watching where he was walking and also watching the faces of the captives.

He stopped three times. The last time was almost within arm's reach of the Texan who showed no interest.

Walt reversed his course and went back the way he had come. Where he stopped for the last time he was on the north side of the rock slab closer to where Damon was leaning on the shovel.

Without a word Walt took the shovel, handed it to Estevan, moved clear and pointed as he said, 'Dig!'

Estevan looked from Walt to the Texan. Lincoln repeated it in Spanish. '*Excavar.*'

There was no sunken place, no earth softer than other soil. When Estevan had hammered at the unrelenting ground the Texan looked at Walt. 'You playin' a game?'

Walt picked up the crowbar, made the *vaquero* give ground and went to work.

The first eight inches were unwilling to yield. As Walt continued to slam the chisel-edged end of the bar into the ground the earth broke into large pieces. He handed the bar to Estevan and said it again, 'Dig!'

The excavating continued with no improvement in visibility but the deeper-down soil broke away more readily. Estevan was breathing harder when the Texan spoke exasperatedly. 'How deep did you fellers bury that cache?'

Walt showed a wintry smile and gave an ambiguous answer. 'Just keep diggin'.'

Damon, the youngest of them, was well muscled. He considered taking

Estevan's place. He had hired out to dig post holes for stockmen and some of the villagers, but Walt told Estevan to hand the tool to his employer and told the Texan to dig, no talk, just dig.

He was not entirely obeyed. Lincoln took the bar, glared at Walt, raised the bar and slammed it into the ground. The shattered earth had rotten croaker cloth on it when it was pulled back for the next strike.

Lincoln eased the bar down carefully, removed soft soil and rotting gunny sacking with it. He peeled off the soil with old cloth on it, examined it and looked at Walt, who was smiling thinly. Lincoln said, 'You buried it in sacking? I hope there isn't any paper money down there.'

Walt answered for the first time in more than an hour in a calm tone of voice.

'There's greenbacks . . . they're in a bottle. From here on be careful with your diggin'. Use the shovel.'

The Texan leaned to look where the

digging had yielded sacking, tossed his tool aside, got down on both knees and gruntingly scooped dirt with his bare hands. He paused once to look up when he asked a question. 'How much is down here?'

Walt's answer was curt. 'Dig!'

Lincoln dug. The next time he leaned back with a two-handed amount of soft soil there was more rotten, damp sackcloth mixed with gold coins. Small ones. Lincoln emptied both hands at the boots of Walt Kimball, and rocked back waiting for Walt to kneel and select coins from the dirt.

Walt grinned at him, lifted out his six-gun, held it no more than eighteen inches from the Texan and repeated himself. 'Dig, you son of a bitch!'

Lincoln had to lean far over to scoop more dirt mixed with coins. He leaned further to dig moist earth away from a quart glass jar of the variety ranch women used to preserve food in.

Damon leaned with both hands on his knees and had no opportunity to jump clear when the Texan hurled the dirt and coins into Damon's face while simultaneously launching himself across the hole at Walt. It was a desperate act and a futile one. Walt's pistol barrel went up and came down in a chopping slash.

Lincoln crumpled, partly in the hole, partly on the ground in front of the marshal.

Estevan was too surprised to move and when he did poise himself to jump up Damon met him, crushed him to the ground and cocked a stone-hard fist.

The *vaquero* made a falsetto yelp and raised both arms to shield himself from being struck.

11

A Long Ride

A pair of bony forearms did not prevent most of the blow from breaking past the shielding arms but the blow was sufficient to cause a high-pitched squeal of pain.

They now had a pair of battered prisoners. One had a cracked forearm and was useless for gouging out soft earth and coins of both silver and gold. Lincoln was half in and half out of the hole.

The *vaquero* sat on the ground rocking back and forth. Walt pulled Lincoln away from the hole and pointed to the *vaquero*. The Mexican cowboy crawled to the huge tan rock and sat there holding his injured arm with one that was not injured.

The time-consuming part was sifting

money from dirt. The sun was well up and climbing before Walt thought they had emptied the cache of coins and greenbacks in bottles including a particularly large bottle with paper curled inside which showed practically no weathering.

The paper inside the largest bottle had a legible note that reiterated what Sam Crawford had written elsewhere: it bequeathed the jar's contents to Damon. It was a long-winded document mentioning Damon several times. Old Sam included an itemized list of things such as saddles, silver-mounted bridles, guns, even a pair of boots Sam had had custom made using a diagram of two large stockinged feet. The diagram had been made of Sam's feet which were much larger.

They cleansed the coins and bottles with Walt watching the prisoners like a hawk. Walt also resolved the matter of transporting everything to the cabin by depriving Estevan of his shirt.

Lincoln found a cache of unused

candles, lit two, put them on the table after pushing the dead *vaquero* off it to the floor.

Damon got a fire going in the wood stove, waited until Walt told him to use someone's old abandoned lass rope to tie the prisoners. Walt sat at the table alternately drying coins with Estevan's filthy shirt and making stacks of money according to denomination and whether they were gold or silver.

Damon had a good fire going by the time he'd dragged the dead *vaquero* out back of a small shed, then rummaged in the rustlers' saddle-bags for tinned goods to make a meal out of.

Eventually the heat outside from sunlight equalled the heat made by the stove, and Damon closed the stove's damper.

Then Damon crossed to the table to sit and watch Walt finish making his mounds of money.

He showed Damon the notes from within the bottles. They were mostly repetitious notes as though old Sam wanted to be sure the right person read them.

The only thing that eased Walt's anxiety, aside from newday warmth, was the scent of bubbling coffee. He got two cupsful and returned to the table smiling. As he sat down with both work-swollen hands around his cup he said, 'Boy, you can buy the settlement if you're of a mind.'

Estevan was groaning. His arm was swollen. He asked Walt if he knew how to make a bandage for his painful arm.

Walt's smile diminished as he left the table to care for the Mexican.

It required time to make a bandage and a sling during which time not a single word passed between Estevan and the more massive *gringo* who groaned as he pushed himself back up to his feet. He was looking at Damon when he said, 'Takes a sight longer gettin' up than it used to.'

Walt stood a moment with the *vaquero* at his feet then let go a long sigh and addressed the bandaged man.

'Boy, you been in bad company.'

Estevan showed an anxious smile when he replied, 'It is for my *esposa* and little ones. He don't say he was going to bring back those cattle by stealing them.'

Walt was rueful. 'But you figured to drive them back. Bought or not. *Si*?'

Estevan switched his attention to Damon. 'The rope is too tight, *señor*.'

Walt groaned as he knelt and removed the binding. He helped the Mexican to sit up. Walt said, 'You put up a pretty good fight for that son of a bitch you work for.'

Lincoln asked to also be set free and Walt shook his head. Damon told Estevan to feed himself and the man he worked for.

For Harry Lincoln it was difficult even after the *vaquero* had hoisted Lincoln into a sitting position supported by a bent knee.

A large animal pushed through underbrush somewhere behind the line shack. The men froze. Their silence

218

made every sound seem louder.

Walt freed-up his sidearm and alternately looked at his companions and the log wall which had no window.

Walt broke the stillness. 'Bear,' he said.

Damon fisted his six-gun as he started for the door. Walt stopped him with a growl. 'Leave it be. If he don't hear us inside he'll go away.'

A horse bawled. It was the sound of a terrified animal unable to get clear. Harry Lincoln spoke. 'That broken door — ' He did not complete the sentence. Everyone eased around. The only thing holding the door was one handmade old iron hinge and it only held because someone had balanced it. All the varmint had to do was come around front. Lincoln addressed his *vaquero* in Spanish. 'Push the table against the door.'

Walt growled. 'Leave the damn door. You push that thing an' he'll hear it . . . just be quiet.'

Damon flattened against the wall

facing the door. He held his six-gun hanging loose, waiting. The critter brushed against the wall. There was no scrub for the bear to break past but as the animal passed he brushed against wood as he continued to move. He stopped moving near the north-east corner and did something only bears did; he reared up on his hind legs to reach the juncture of the wall and the punky wood of the meagre overlap where the roof met the point of juncture between the roof and the wall.

Walt said, 'Lincoln! Get closer. He's goin' to break through where he's tearing.'

The Texan put a wry look in Walt's direction. 'An' when he comes through what am I supposed to do, slap him in the face?'

Walt was accustomed to being in charge. Lincoln was humiliated because he had no gun. He stood fast as he said, 'If you're feelin' real brave trade places with me.'

The discussion ended abruptly when

a large hairy forefoot came through where the rotting wood was punkiest.

Walt fired from over by the stove, hair flew as did punky wood and the large paw pulled back beyond sight. At the same moment the bear let go with a bawl that could have been heard a fair distance. This noise was followed by a threshing sound as the attacker fell in a thicket wailing and blundering.

If there was a second bear, it wasted no time in jumping up in one of those clumsy running gaits that were unique to their kind.

Walt punched the Texan out of his path as he crossed the room in an angry charge.

Damon had stiffened against the west wall, handgun cocked and ready. As the lawman passed, Damon yelled at him, 'Get belly down!'

It was sound advice that the marshal did not need. He fell against the rotten wall where blood and broken bits of loft wall, soiled brown hair and deep scratch indentations mingled.

How badly Walt's shot had injured his furry adversary no one could say; bears were the biggest cry-babies in anyone's forested uplands.

The aroma of burnt gunpowder was strong in the shack until the bear scent and daylight exceeded it.

The men had to assume the bear had abandoned his scented search. They were satisfied to remain quiet. They listened to the injured predator noisily leaving the area making no attempt to retreat in silence.

Damon kicked away the ruined door, got past it out into the shadowy trees looking for a wounded hairy creature whose inclination was flight.

When he returned to the cabin there was an unattended six-gun at the table with men around it on benches offering Walt advice on the repairing of a torn hand.

Walt picked up the six-gun, shoved it in the front of his britches and went to the stove for more coffee. Damon used what remained of the shirt to bundle all the money, jars and papers from the cache and used stout twine to secure his inheritance. Estevan's geniality deepened toward his captors and while awaiting Walt's return with the coffee, stove heat warmed Damon and the *vaquero*. They became sufficiently close to exchange occasional words.

This was the only show of friendliness. Walt told Damon in English the *vaquero* was being friendly because Walt and Damon had the upper hand.

Damon shrugged.

Walt was concerned with getting back down out of the uplands. Walt told Damon to stay inside while Walt went to feed the saddle stock and make preparations for the long ride back.

Damon briefly hesitated and nodded agreement. The reason for his delay was a matter that had arisen another time; as owner who had hired Walt as his range boss it was his position to give orders, not Walt's right, so although he nodded agreement he privately made up his mind that when they were down out of the highlands he and Walt would have an understanding about who was boss.

Walt may have surmised something about this because when Damon made no move to leave the shack, Walt started toward the door. For Damon the question of who was the hired man came up. He spoke as Walt reached the door. 'You stay in here with our claim-jumpers. I'll tend to the horses.'

Again they exchanged a long look before Walt grumbled something, got the ruined door open and stood beside it as Damon moved.

Where they passed, Marshal Kimball softly said, 'You're head Indian . . . be careful out there. This time of year bears travel in pairs.'

Walt propped the door after Damon, stood listening until he was satisfied then went back as far as the rickety table with the weighty bundle atop it.

Harry Lincoln had watched until the door had been closed then said, 'I been worryin' over an idea. How's it come when the boy says jump you say how high?'

Walt answered almost indifferently. 'Everything in that bundle belongs to him. I'm a hired man. I hired on as range boss . . . that satisfy you?'

Lincoln said, 'Untie me. There's enough on that there table for both of us to split it down the middle an' go back to Texas an' live like kings.'

Walt's expression did not change. 'Let me tell you somethin', mister. That old man who had the cache up here under the grave of that old Indian who is fallin' to pieces atop that tombstone . . . him an' me was right close . . . like brothers. Me'n old Sam Crawford was that close . . . closer in fact. I give old Sam my word before he died I'd make damned sure the boy would inherit every damned cent along with the ranch, all the cattle an' horses, whichever of us died first. Sam died, Mr Lincoln. Everything belongs to the boy . . . everything.'

The Texan put his head to one side

and narrowed his eyes. 'Everything?'

Walt glared. 'If you been figurin' you'n me'd split it you're talkin' to the wrong man. Set down an' keep quiet. If the boy don't come back — '

Lincoln interrupted. 'He'll come back. Anyone hung with that much luck will come back. What interests me is what you figure to do with us survivors? It depends on you, Mr Lawman.'

The Texan leaned on the table beside the bundle eyeing Walt Kimball. After a while he softly said, 'Mister, you're as crazy as a pet 'coon.'

Walt returned to his earlier place, swilled a cupful of coffee, took it to one of the bunks and sat down looking into the cup without saying another word.

The Texan had more to say, 'Mister, you're older than me. I'd guess you got maybe another ten, twelve years to go. Half of that loot will take care of you right up to the end. Livin' right well. Maybe get you a woman who can cook . . . an' maybe have a pup or two.'

Walt's mouth barely lifted in a cold

smile. 'I never saw the woman I'd like to get hitched to, and kids . . . just plain never liked 'em.'

When Damon returned, the pair of older men were drinking coffee in silence. Walt filled a cup and handed it to Damon. As the younger man accepted the cup he said, 'That bear wasn't very big. I'd guess a tad less than half grown.'

Walt put his cup aside and jerked his head in the Texan's direction. 'Come along, Texas. You know anything about bears? That was a cub we scairt off. Cubs stay with their mothers sometimes as long as two years'n longer. If the old girl is out there . . . ' Walt jerked his head again and walked towards the door.

Lincoln did not hesitate. Where he came from it was settled territory. Bear-sightings were not common, but neither were they unheard of.

At the door, Lincoln mentioned being unarmed and Walt gave him a small grin. 'I'll be with you. Come on.

Damon, don't let those left behind get near a weapon.'

It was late in the day. Smoke-shaded clouds were drifting, indifferently, moving in front of a thinning moon. It was quiet until the older men were passing close to the corral, then they were nickered at. One animal, probably the critter who had been noisy earlier, stood in line behind the lodgepole stringers and nickered.

Walt halted; the ground was bare where feed had been pitched earlier. He gestured for his companion to pitch in a few more forksful.

The Texan obeyed, leaned on the hay fork looking at the horses when Walt said, 'Come along.'

It was Walt's idea to go north which was the direction that young bear had taken. He halted to listen. The bear who had torn at the cabin had gone in that direction limping and whimpering.

The Texan almost stumbled over a fallen limb. He picked it up to use as a cane and kept on walking. They reached one of those places where the injured bear had sat down to lick its bleeding foot when Lincoln took three wide steps to get closer and swung the deadfall he had been using as a cane.

Walt had not been watching from where he stopped and took the strike alongside the head and on the shoulder.

Walt, who was in mid stride, almost lost his footing and tried to face around as the limb was raised for another strike.

Lincoln instinctively went for the six-gun that wasn't there with one hand, while lunging to get closer when he tried using the club again.

Walt sidestepped as the limb descended. Lincoln got clear and tried to swing again. Walt felt the club graze one arm and swiftly turned away.

The Texan let go of the club and lunged face first. This time Walt was coming in and took the blow head on. It jarred him to a halt. Walt had survived his share of barroom brawls and twisted to avoid the strike, got settled squarely on both legs and kicked as hard as he could.

Lincoln faltered, recovered and Walt got poised for another kick. This one connected with a knee. The Texan staggered, caught himself and limped sideways at the same time Walt fired his right fist.

The Texan was jolted, regained his balance and swung a ham-sized fist that Walt had expected and sucked back, took a solid stance as Lincoln leaned in behind his next strike. It missed by inches. As Walt sprang clear, the Texan jumped ahead ready for the next strike.

This one connected and Walt's legs wobbled.

Lincoln fired off two strikes in succession and yielded ground.

Walt did not follow up, his legs were still wobbly so when the next blow came Walt was caught unprepared.

He went down like a pole-axed bull and didn't feel the boot toe driven hard into his side.

The Texan had Walt's gun aimed and

cocked when Walt shook clear of the fuzziness and rolled to get upright. He didn't make it. The next kick was harder. Walt dropped flat sucking air.

The Texan took several backward steps and let go with another kick. This time Walt lost his breath and sank flat down.

Walt heard words but distantly as the other man dropped to one knee to swing a blow that could not miss his adversary. Walt waited with a balled fist ready, paused until the last moment, then hit the Texan who leaned perfectly still before he went over sideways.

Walt was as nearly unconscious as he had ever been in his life. He went to a rotting stump and sat down to gingerly massage his body where it hurt.

His thoughts were unclear but where he sat, replaying all over it, helped him recover. When his breathing recovered he ransacked the pockets of the Texan, brought forth a thick roll of currency, half a palm-load of coins and a crumpled envelope addressed to the

Texan which more than likely had been picked up *en route* by the Texan.

Walt pocketed what he confiscated, sat awhile until his aches and pains settled where they would remain for a week or so, before he went for the horses, left one tied to a tree where it would be available when the Texan came around, mounted his own horse and turned back the way he had come.

When the man propped against a tree back yonder came round he would have a choice, either track Walt back to the line shack or ride northward the way he and Walt had been heading.

With no idea how far they had come nor how far it was to get back he watered the horse at a creek and with daylight fading dug out the letter and read it.

It was written in Spanish. Walt disgustedly shoved it back in a pocket, dismounted when he caught the scent of smoke and led the animal.

With time to think he considered the worst possibility. If Damon got careless with his new friend, the Mex cowboy called Estevan, there was a possibility that Estevan would have gotten a gun and with the loot recovered from where old Sam Crawford and Walt had cached Sam's savings he would by now be south of the settlement and still going.

For some reason Walt's legs stopped hurting so he got back astride and concentrated on the scent of wood smoke.

When he had left the shack everything edible had been eaten. He reined to a halt behind the corral, swung off, left his horse tied back a ways and was standing beside it speculating on how to approach the house when an animal bawled. It had not been a horse, possibly a burro or a mule. It had unquestionably caught the scent of Walt's animal, or possibly of Walt himself.

He stood with his horse, motionless and jockeying for scent and noise. The critter did not repeat its buglelike bawling. This time Walt was prepared and not only yanked loose the tie-down over his beltgun but also moved to his left, which was westerly, where one of the Mexicans had been encountered before.

He was soundless and prepared. When he had candlelight in sight he kept to his left until he heard a large animal shuffling its feet, the way thirsty or hungry animals did who wanted something they could not reach.

Both Walt and his horse were also dry and hungry.

Having established the direction he moved very carefully toward it. What he saw was the unkempt rump of a mule. It was tied closer to the back of the line shack. He continued to move and stopped when the animal scuffed dust as it attempted to see behind itself.

Walt belonged to that unusual breed of men who did not wear spurs. When he was close enough he softly spoke and the long-eared critter turned its head as far as its tether would permit. It stopped faunching, stood perfectly motionless and allowed Walt to stroke its neck.

It was not only thin but it was also rough-coated with ribs showing. It liked the stroking, but from its scrawny appearance it probably would have liked something to eat more.

Its saddle was an old McClellan, scarred and unkempt. There was a bedroll behind the skimpy cantle and someone had rigged it with fenders which it hadn't been made with.

There was a saddle boot on the right side with no carbine in it. Whoever owned the mule hadn't fed it lately and had taken his carbine with him into the line shack. Rangemen drew conclusions about other rangemen from the way they treated their animals and they carried their weapons. In this case Walt Kimball who had been a man-hunting lawman for a good part of his life drew a pair of conclusions. Riding the mule to skin and bones meant the man had kept on the move. Taking his Winchester into the house with him supported his other presumption.

He removed the cinch on both sides and tossed it away. Whatever happened from here on the visitor would be unable to jump into his saddle. If he had an excuse for being inside, Walt would explain about the cinch-less saddle and apologize.

He was still hungry but he was no longer weary.

He took as much time as was required to stalk around the house. It was getting along toward dusk so there was no point in trying to read boot tracks.

He was tempted to cut the mule's tie shank but he didn't. The clearing was shy of things a man might stumble over or rattle when he walked through and his earlier annoyance about underbrush was now something to be thankful about.

The dusk was settling with the slowness that usually accompanied it so he was able to get around front. He kept a decent distance between himself and the broken door.

With the passing of time the dusk deepened and there was an occasional exchange of words that Walt could distinguish. Damon's voice had a slightly higher pitch.

Once anger made the deeper voice sound louder. Whoever he was he snarled when he said, 'Come on, boy, no one takes that long to . . . ' The mule brayed. It startled Walt. It probably had the same effect on the men inside because there was absolute silence until the man with the deeper voice said, 'Gawddammit, boy, he's out there. That mule don't squawl for nothin'.'

Damon answered curtly. 'How about bein' hungry, mister? I grew up around mules.'

The man interrupted. He sounded disgusted. 'You said he'd be back directly. It's been better'n an hour. Maybe close to two hours.'

If Damon answered Walt didn't hear him.

Walt straightened his crouch, flexed

his legs and decided to move. It would be dark directly.

Coincidences were rare but this time Walt was straightening up to his full height when the broken door made an unearthly racket and some broken bits of wood fell outward.

Walt dropped flat and held his breath. He had a good sighting of the mule-man. He hadn't been near a razor in a long time. It wasn't just the full, thick beard but the hair on both sides of his face that fell forward before he could toss his head to clear his face.

He was tall, thin as a snake, his shirt was torn and filthy. He sprang sideways. Walt had seen enough. The man's gauntness was most noticeable. Of his features Walt's glimpse was too brief.

There was a loud clatter inside the cabin. Walt heard the man's fierce profanity at the same time as one of the homemade benches hit the intruder in the shoulders from behind.

Walt didn't shoot. He sprang upright and charged. The broken wood nearly upset him. Damon looked up and aimed a kick. Walt heard the breath go out of the man's throat.

Damon was heavy enough. The kick helped. The intruder did not try for his weapon, he curled and gasped.

Walt got a fistful of filthy shirt and hoisted. The intruder came half off the floor before the shirt tore.

Damon finished the lifting and slammed the old man against the wall on the left side of the shattered door.

Walt caught the man from behind with both arms and, raising his leg halfway, slammed his knee into the man's back propelling him to the table where he fell.

Walt eased up. The intruder had no fight left in him. He called out that he quit, wrestled around until he could stand and slumped on the table.

Walt got a stool, shoved it at him and told Damon to stand behind the old man.

Without a gun the stranger was harmless. He peered from little piggy eyes across the table from Walt and said, 'So you *was* out there. I knew you'd be. My name's Eliah Crockett. I'm from way off down south. One of the Crocketts that got his throat cut at the mud fort in Texas. Mister, you got anythin' to eat?'

Walt shook his head, looked at the man who was older than Walt had originally thought and said, 'How'd you come to be here?'

'I got lost comin' across them mountains northerly.' The old man went to the stove to lift a lid and expectorate. As he moved back he said, 'That's my last cud. I been chewin' it off an' on since yestiddy.'

The old man punched the shirt bundle and wrinkled his nose. 'Messican,' he said. 'I'd know that smell a mile off.'

Walt settled back looking at Eliah Crockett. He knew about that other Crockett. Just about everyone did. He looked at Damon. 'You thought he was me comin' back?'

'Yes. There's some burnt sardine meat in that pan on the floor by the stove.'

Walt stood up. 'Give it to him,' he said, and lifted the bundled shirt. 'Saddle us up, Damon. We can be down at . . . your house come morning.'

Damon didn't move until Walt grinned and wagged his head. 'I keep forgettin', you're the boss.'

Damon smiled. 'I'll rig 'em out. You visit with old windbag and Estevan. I'm tired of this upland country.'

12

The Montanans

Eliah Crockett was indeed harmless without his weapon, and for a fact he was a windbag. After Damon left the line shack Eliah regaled the men inside with stories about Davy Crockett. He insisted that his kinsman lowered the bear population where he settled before going to Texas and the Alamo. Eliah spent as much time as he could recounting Davy's death at the hands of the Mexicans when The Alamo fell. Walt and the others had no alternative to listening and avoided stirring up the scrawny old man by denying that he could know the details of the killing because Eliah had not been in The Alamo that last day otherwise he would have been killed along with all the defenders, who were killed to a man.

It was totally dark when Damon appeared at the ruined door trailing a fistful of reins in one hand. Walt said, 'Took you long enough, boy,' and Damon answered just as crisply. 'Fed his mule first. There ought to be a law against folks treatin' animals the way he treated that mule. You ready to ride, Walt?'

The older man did not reply, he was irritable. Eliah Crockett stopped in front of his mule. Its ribs still showed but its paunch was devoid of wrinkles. Eliah said, 'The lad's taken care of you. Now let's see if you can be rode for a while.'

As Eliah went to the left side of his animal to mount, the mule let him get his left foot in the stirrup then laid back its ears and bit Eliah hard on the ham. Eliah exploded in pain and anger. He and the mule very clearly had no liking for each other.

Walt smiled from the saddle. His attitude improved as he led off with Damon behind him using his left hand to balance the shirting bundle which was an awkward load.

They stopped when they saw the Texan, who, not wanting to be out where the bear or bears might be and hurting from his beating from Walt, had made his way back to the line shack. Walt stopped long enough to tie his hands before resuming their ride.

The Texan and his Mexican, with wrists tied to their saddle horn, were silent for part of the ride.

The closer the group got to level country the quieter they became and remained, until Lincoln eased up closer to Walt and said something about the cattle for which old Sam had given him a bill of sale.

Walt's retort was the result of considerable pondering. He asked to see the bill of sale which Lincoln could not produce with both wrists made fast to his saddle horn.

They stopped. Walt reined close to the Texan and asked which pocket the bill of sale was in.

Lincoln scowled. 'Small shirt pocket behind and inside the bigger one. But you got to free up my hands before I can reach it.'

Walt's stirrup brushed the Texan's stirrup as he leaned perilously and grabbed Lincoln's shirt.

He hadn't intended to tear the shirt pocket but his lunging hand tore the pocket's flap. Lincoln squawked and tried to back away. Walt kept pressing close. Walt cursed, groped fiercely and straightened in his saddle clutching a soiled and crumpled scrap of paper. When he had the paper he reined clear, got close to Damon and handed him the paper.

Lincoln bawled like a bay steer. For all the good it did him he might just as well have bayed at the moon.

Damon told Walt to hold up and tried to smooth the paper so it could be read.

He looked at Walt and grinned as he offered Walt the bill of sale. Walt took it, had to seek enough light to read it by and afterward handed it back to Damon. 'Chew it up,' Walt said.

They resumed their passage with Damon chewing the paper to a soggy lump. He turned his head to jettison the unreadable mess and expectorated it.

Lincoln said, 'I'll swear to a magistrate standin' on a Bible.'

Walt smiled. 'An' we'll swear it never existed.'

It was cold by the time they had the rooftop of old Sam Crawford's barn in sight. The Texan had ridden the last few miles behind Walt and in front of Damon. Someone had bunched cattle north-west of old Sam's ranch yard. Walt took this clear meaning of ownership to signify that someone was putting in a claim. He waited until they were in the Crawford yard before taking Damon to one side to tell him he thought he knew who had staked that claim on the cattle whose owner was dead. Walt helped Damon chain their three prisoners and went out to catch a fresh horse. They left the yard riding in the direction of the village.

Bunched cattle meant someone was fixing to have a cattle drive. With the Texans out of it, that left the Montanans who handled cattle stolen below the border and sold over the line into Canada.

Those bunched cattle hadn't had time to spread and scatter. Walt's pondering left him convinced that the Crawford-branded cattle they had seen back yonder were going to be started up the trail very soon. It was past supper-time when he rode into the village. There was not a soul in sight. He tied up front of the jailhouse and had his hand on the latch string when he heard the distant bawling of cattle. It wasn't the sound of milk cows, it was the bellowing of hungry range cattle.

He left the village riding westerly in the direction of that bawling. He was sure of what he would find: those bawling critters were either hungry or thirsty. Walt believed they were hungry and he was right. The corrals which had held cattle before when Walt had been out there were once again fairly full of range cattle. At least half of them were belted, and every one of them was tucked up. Walt decided they had been corralled since early in the day. He sat his horse watching the milling animals.

Every one of the cattle carried old Sam Crawford's brand.

He dismounted, opened the gate and stood aside as the cattle fought among themselves to get out. There wasn't much feed but they dropped their heads and cropped whatever they found.

Night-time favoured most of what the town marshal did after emptying that set of holding corrals. The cattle began to spread and wander.

As far as the town marshal was concerned, if the cattle could graze off the territory northerly, which was in the direction where they belonged, all the better.

He rode back to town to roust out possemen. He had only had to do this twice before during his long tenure as the local lawman.

Bud Otten was the blacksmith and wheelwright, a widower who lived behind his shop.

When Walt routed him out of bed the blacksmith scratched his head and blinked his eyes as he listened to what Walt Kimball had to say and began wagging his head before Walt was finished, to say, 'Ain't been nobody wantin' fresh shoes on their saddle animals in more'n a week. Walt, I'm not even sure I've seen any Montanans. Yeah, I heard about Sam bein' found in some brush with a busted head. Are you sure about what you been sayin?'

Walt was sure. 'Three of 'em, Bud. If they're fixin' to drive old Sam's cattle upcountry, them rustlers is bedded down somewhere around.'

Otten considered his old friend. 'Maybe I can't help you, Walt.'

The marshal removed his hat, scratched and asked if the blacksmith had seen any Crawford cattle. The blacksmith sat on the edge of his cot looking at the floor. 'It's late,' he exclaimed. 'Are you plumb sure of all this, Walt?'

The town marshal answered curtly. 'Dollar a day, Bud. Posseman's pay.'

Otten said, 'Kick them boots over to me.'

After Walt had briefly watched the blacksmith stamp into his boots, stand up and reach for his shirt, britches, and shellbelted six-gun, he said, 'Go askin' around, Bud. I'm goin' to roust up Buck Thorne.'

The bull-built horseshoer was cinching up his belts when he said, 'For a fact, Walt. If there's fellers bedded down Buck might know. As nosy as he is he'd know better'n anyone about strangers in town. I'll rig up my animal, try to round up some men an' wait for you out front.'

Walt scarcely heeded the settling night. He was anxious about finding the Montanans before sun-up, which was normally the time stockmen moved cattle when they started a drive.

The storekeeper was an individual who opened his store early because he closed it early.

He lived in only the second residence in the village that was painted. Rousting him out was less difficult than it had been to get the horseshoer awake.

In some ways the storekeeper was the opposite of the blacksmith. Buck Thorne was well over six feet tall and was as skinny as a snake, with a mop of jet-black hair he continually used his left hand to push out of his face, and while Bud Otten the smith was reticent, particularly when he was working, the storekeeper ran off at the mouth as though he suffered from verbal dysentery.

Walt had no sooner awakened Thorne than he began shooting questions at the town marshal.

Walt tried to cut him off after explaining what he wanted and why he wanted it.

The storekeeper got dressed and took

Walt into his parlour carrying a tumbler three-quarters full of water as they walked along. He sat the tumbler down and while Walt was explaining Thorne used two fingers to fish a pair of false teeth out of the water glass and implant them.

He knew about the strangers, and launched into a long-winded description of each one starting out with a Texan accompanied by a pair of beaners from below the border. Thorne's description was faultless and he had only seen them twice.

Walt worked the conversation around to the Montanans, and described the one Montanan he remembered best, a sheriff named Jeff Cutler.

That stopped the talkative storekeeper in midsentence. His eyes widened, his breath seemed to have stopped and he clawed at the arms of the chair where he was sitting. 'Walt, for Chris'sake, why didn't you mention him sooner!'

Thorne came out of his chair as though he had sat upon a coiled spring.

'The name's wrong but the description fits Mr Jones to a T.'

Thorne's startled reaction cleared the marshal's head of a descending tiredness that had begun to settle hours earlier.

Thorne said, 'Come with me,' and left the house with his shirt-tail flapping.

Walt got abreast and, as the pair of them ran, Walt yelled, 'What in hell's wrong with you?'

Thorne answered breathlessly. 'Upstairs . . . hurry!'

Buck Thorne whipped northward past two buildings he owned, came to an intersecting unkempt alley and ran southward until he reached the rear door of his store. He already had the key in his fist when they stopped and Thorne fought briefly with the locked door before throwing it wide open. So far open in fact that the door slammed into a wall.

The stairs were to Thorne's left. Walt was ready to run up the stairs when his companion ran past, grabbed two candle stands and was in the act of lighting both candles when Walt said, 'Leave it dark!'

The storekeeper had already succeeded in lighting the candles and turned slowly holding both candles as high as his shoulders. He stopped so abruptly Walt nearly collided with him.

Thorne yelled, 'Look there! They broke the hasp off the gun rack . . . an' there, for Gawd's sake . . . they've taken tinned food.'

Walt eased past with one of the candles, stopped midway, slowly raised the light and quietly said, 'That was them, Buck. Sure as I'm standin' here.'

Thorne went to an old bench, sat down and raised both hands to his face. Through his fingers he said, 'They said they was cattle buyers. They had plenty of money to make up a goodly sized drive.'

Walt went heavily up the stairs. A frail cotton shade that Thorne's wife had insisted upon draping over the upstairs window had been torn loose and dropped on the floor. Walt lingered long enough to be satisfied the men who had hired the room had spent very little time in it. He went back downstairs and found the proprietor standing behind a long counter holding an empty cotton bag he had recovered. He faced Walt Kimball when he said, 'Cleaned me out, Walt. See this little bag? My wife made it for me to put the money in that I'd take down to the bank when it was full enough.'

Thorne dramatically upended the little sack and shook it. Not even dust emerged.

Someone, undoubtedly attracted by candlelight inside the store, was banging on the roadway door with a fist.

When it became evident that Buck Thorne was going to ignore the hammering, Walt went to open the door and the blacksmith met him with a scowl. 'You said out front,' Otten exclaimed.

Walt left the door open and jerked his

head as he turned away.

Within moments the blacksmith gauged the loss, the owner's reaction and stood with Walt as he spoke in little more than a whisper. 'Old Benitez saw them bed down in the old mission.'

Walt eyed the speaker. Time was passing. If the Montanans meant to push the corralled animals northerly to mingle with the scattering loose stock and then start the total drive they would not waste time.

Cattle, unlike horses, could not be pushed in a mileslong run, particularly if any of the cows were heavy with calf. And for a fact there had been bulls with the cows.

He told the blacksmith to stay at the store while he took the beanpole storekeeper with him and led off easterly past houses and shacks. The storekeeper led Walt past an impressive structure. The house was large and had a number of sheep and goat sheds and pens on its south side. What wood had been used for the sheds appeared to have come from the old mission. There were two complete sheds, even their roofs were in good shape. The storekeeper made a wide scout out and around the ruins.

As Walt sought men, the storekeeper went far out until he found three horses standing where an old spring had been developed to give water.

Thorne located Walt, took him where the well was and the pair of them ran the horses as far as they could which would put the wanted men on foot.

In country like they were in catching spooked saddle stock would be difficult, and without horses under them no one would be able to overtake free-running animals.

Walt took the storekeeper with him to the one pen where four walls and a roof provided the kind of hideout Walt was seeking.

It was possible that the bedded-down men would be awakened by the noise of running horses despite the considerable distance the waterhole was from the sheds where men could be sleeping.

There was an increasing chill in the air.

While they were waiting, the store-keeper worried out loud about the blacksmith being alone at his store.

Walt shrugged that off. He had known the blacksmith for many years. Even assuming the sleeping Montanans were awakened by the sound of running horses, it was unlikely they would risk going back to town.

What he told the thin man was that the pair of them could face back around and if the Montanans came running after their horses they could shoot the legs out from under them.

A hurrying figure materialized rattling pieces of sundried, hardened adobe scraps, making no attempt to be quiet. Walt saw him first and discreetly brayed like a sheep. The hurrying shadow stopped stone still and softly called, 'Walt? Marshal Kimball?'

Walt and his companion almost stopped breathing for as long as was required for Walt to identify the voice and respond. 'What in hell are you doin' out here!' The burly blacksmith came forward in a noisy, flat-footed walk that annoyed Walt; shards rattled under his feet.

'For Chris'sake, tiptoe! Did you leave anyone back in the store?'

The answer was returned softly. It had nothing to do with the question. 'Walt? You all right?'

Walt growled in exasperation. 'Come up here, an' quit crackin' them scraps when you walk.'

Buck Thorne slithered closer to the marshal and said, 'Who'n hell is he?'

Walt gave a disgusted answer. 'It's your friend the horseshoer. The feller we left back yonder keepin' watch.'

Otten snorted and addressed the dark-shadowed individuals facing him.

'After you fellers left there wasn't no reason for me to wait around. Walt, you found 'em?'

Instead of answering, Walt jerked his head in the direction of the shed that hadn't fallen apart and cautioned both his companions about being quiet. Walt showed them how to do it, he went far out and around the ruin and approached the shed from the east.

Where he halted he held up his left hand for the other two to stop, and lifted out his sidearm with his right hand.

The shed was almost entirely adobe. If there had been any wood used in its construction it had to be inside.

The blacksmith seemed barely to move as he passed Walt, stopped stone still for a long moment before turning to beckon the other men.

When the three of them were close enough they understood why he had stopped in this particular spot.

Someone inside the shed was snoring.

13

A Settled Claim

There was a sound of movement, of a man stifling a cough. Walt went close to the door. Inside a man cleared his throat and heaved heavily to his feet. Walt took his final steps and was silhouetted in the opening with his right hand rising. The man inside faced around and asked for a name. He got it.

'Walt Kimball.' The shadowed man raised his voice. 'Too late — '

Walt's gunhand moved with grace. 'You son of a bitch!'

The Montanan's voice held a thin strand of patience when he replied. 'It'd be you!'

The shadow opposite him twisted and moved one hand. The difference was almost too slight to be seen. The guns seemed to explode simultaneously.

Not quite. The man in darkest gloom lost a moment of his shifting stance. The gunshots awakened everyone in the village who slept lightly. The gun fell heavily and loudly. There was no need for a third shot, but two men came swiftly from different directions. The third man was either crouching or stumbling to his right side of the door. He was on one knee with his six-gun lightly balanced. No one came forward in the darkness but someone inside where it was darker called suddenly and violently. 'Jeff! Jeff!'

The answer came from outside westerly. 'Come out. No guns. Be real careful!'

The caller tried again, his word trailing off for lack of answer. 'Jeffff!'

The running men came to a dust-scattering halt. They were close enough to see the town marshal's outline. One of them said, 'Who's in there? Gawd-dammit, sound off!'

The answer was accented. 'It is me in here. Who are you?'

The answer did not come from Walt but the words were the same. 'Come out. You got five seconds. Leave your guns inside. *Move. Damn you! Now!* One stick of dynamite'll blow you'n the house to hell an' back!'

There was no explosive but the word worked. Two sidearms thumped on the rock-hard adobe floor with the men who had dropped them coming out slowly. One had his boots on, the other man didn't. Their arms were over their heads.

As Walt arose from his kneeling position, the storekeeper and the blacksmith came closer with their handguns aimed and cocked.

The blacksmith addressed his companion from the side of his mouth.

'Buck, there's another one.'

Walt passed inside, grunted as he stumbled and said, 'Not this one. Half his head's blown away.' In a softer tone Walt said, 'I didn't aim that high. I'll drag him out. Get out of the way.'

Buck Thorne the storekeeper turned

away. The blacksmith went around picking up weapons.

The surviving cattle dealers from up north considered the men holding guns. One of them addressed Kimball. 'You was with that tousled-headed kid. We ain't done nothin'.'

Walt answered. 'Nobody said you did. Them corralled cattle; we turned 'em loose. It's one hell of a long way up to Montana. Start walkin'!'

The second Montanan said, 'How about him?'

Walt leathered his six-gun. 'Carry him with you.'

The man standing nearest to the dead man said, 'Like hell. We got three horses, mister.'

'You *had* three horses. The way they was runnin' the last time I saw 'em they're halfway to the Mex border.'

One of the Montanans jutted his jaw in the direction of the dead man when he said, 'Search him. I've known him a long time. He don't even go out to pee without a wad of money.'

The Montanan was right. The black-smith knelt to do what the storekeeper had no stomach for and arose with a flat packet of greenbacks secured by a horseshoe nail from which the sharp end had been filed smooth.

Walt took the money, peeled off several notes of fairsized denomination, handed them to the rustlers and pointed to their defunct employer as he said, 'Bury him. He belongs to you gents. Pile a mound of these old adobe bricks from the mission. Do whatever you want, he belongs to you. Then buy a couple of horses from the folks around here an' leave. If you want some advice, don't never come back down here or so help me, we'll hang you so high birds wouldn't make nests in your hair.'

Walt pushed up a death's-head smile and jerked his head. 'Start walkin'. Take this carrion with you.'

One of the Montanans looked for-lornly at his companion. 'Take his feet and I'll take his arms. The biggest pile of these old bricks is yonder.'

Walt looked for something to sit on as the pair of Montanans began dragging the dead man. He ended up going inside and pulling out an old rickety bench. As he sat he fished for the makings and passed them around. Only Buck Thorne the storekeeper did not use tobacco. He did not want to wait until the mound had been piled over the dead man but the blacksmith scowled ominously when he said he thought the merchant should wait, and wait he did.

By the time their employer was buried as far beneath as nearly a man-high mound the night was getting well along.

The storekeeper was hungry and suggested going to his store for tinned food to which Walt and the blacksmith agreed, but possibly because the blacksmith knew the storekeeper, he volunteered to go along. Walt told the blacksmith to bring back some horses for the Montanans and a horse for him.

By the time the absent men had returned with tinned goods and mounts, there was a hint of very pale light off in the east and the mound was finished.

The storekeeper offered for sale two army mules he had taken in exchange for delinquent accounts at his store. He put the exact price on them that Walt had given to the dead man's companions.

One Montanan handed over the money and glowered. Walt got astride, nodded around and headed for the Crawford place and its owner who had been guarding prisoners.

He was about half a mile from the Crawford yard when he met Damon riding a roan horse and looking unhappy. The younger man said, 'They got loose, got horses and rode north.'

Walt sat perfectly still. 'Got loose? Damon, how could they get loose when they was chained an' you had the only gun?'

Damon had to fight his roan horse to

stand still, it was one of those fidgeting horses that seemed unable to stand still. While Damon was irritably making the roan to quit squirming he said, 'Well, all I know was that — '

'You fell asleep!'

The roan did not move but it was hunching up to go sideways when Damon made a big show of forcing the animal to stand quietly.

Walt ignored the cake-walking horse. 'They got your gun?'

'Well, not exactly. I felt somethin' cold in my ear an' it was — '

'Your six-gun!'

'Walt, didn't you ever be so damned tired . . . I stoked up a fire . . . '

Walt slumped in the saddle. 'Did you find something to eat?'

'Yeah. After they was gone. You want to ride back? There's plenty to eat.' Damon was tightening his reins when he finished speaking. 'What'd you do in town?'

Walt snorted. 'Town! Folks back there could sleep through the Second

Coming.' Walt squeezed his horse. It began moving. Damon's fidgety roan took that as his cue. He turned, fell in beside Walt's horse and walked along as though he had never intended doing anything else.

When they reached the yard, Walt said, 'Boy, you got a lot to learn. Don't never leave a house empty with candles burnin'.'

While they were unsaddling in the yard Walt explained everything that had happened since he and Damon had last seen each other.

After feeding the animals in the corral they went to the house which was warm, too warm in fact for a man well enough along to be susceptible to the dying oak fire Damon had also fed burls into.

Damon piled a platter with food and put it in front of Walt after which he steered the town marshal into old Sam's cold bed and got him rolled in without his hat or boots. Damon returned to the kitchen, made himself another pot of black coffee laced with whiskey and resumed going through a thick satchel of old Sam's personal and private property, right up until a slight chill arrived when he fed more oak into both the stove and the fireplace, made himself another coffee-whiskey tankardful, and with his back to the fire dropped forward to sleep until someone with very cold fingers shook him awake.

Walt's eyes were puffy, other than that he looked rested and more relaxed.

Damon drew off two cups of black java and returned to the table. As he sat down he said, 'We got to talk, Walt.'

Walt nodded as he sipped the bitter coffee waiting for Damon to say what he had to say.

Finally, Damon gave a big sigh and said, 'Walt, you know why I hung around you'n your office so much?'

Walt shook his head while eyeing the cup of coffee. 'Lonely, boy?'

'Well, that too, but Walt you was nice to me an' I wanted to belong. I wanted a family. Bein' an orphan, sort of, never set well with me.'

Walt remained silent, figuring Damon needed to get things out of his system.

'What I'm tryin' to say . . . Walt, I'm offerin' you half of the ranch. We'll be partners . . . '

Walt had just taken a sip of coffee when that bombshell fell. He managed to finally get it swallowed then said, 'Boy, that's mighty generous. You sure you want to do that? I'd be happy just to work for you.'

'I'm sure, Walt. I think we'd make a good team . . . an' like you said, I got a lot to learn.' Damon went on to say, 'An' we can be sort of like family . . . '

Walt leaned back grinning. 'Boy, you needed a family an' so help you, boy, you got one. All at once you got one.'

Walt held out a roughened hand, Damon smiled and took it. Their powerful handshake lasted until Walt said, 'Well, boy, since we're partners now, what d'you think about us gettin' to work?'

Damon nodded and they started for the door.

Damon stopped, winked at Walt, and went back to blow out the candles.

THE END

Caleb Brett liked his job as deputy sheriff and being betrothed to the sheriff's daughter, Rose. What he didn't like was the thought of the sheriff moving in with them once they were married. But capturing the infamous outlaw Gil Bannerman offered a way out because there was plenty of reward money. Then came Brett's big mistake — he lost Bannerman and was framed. Now everything he treasured was lost. Did he have a chance in hell of fighting his way back?